THE TASTE OF SALT

ALSO BY Martha Southgate

Another Way to Dance
The Fall of Rome
Third Girl from the Left

The Taste of Salt

A NOVEL BY

Martha Southgate

ALGONQUIN BOOKS OF CHAPEL HILL 2011

Published by
ALGONQUIN BOOKS OF CHAPEL HILL
Post Office Box 2225
Chapel Hill, North Carolina 27515-2225

a division of
Workman Publishing
225 Varick Street
New York, New York 10014

Printed in the United States of America.
Published simultaneously in Canada by Thomas Allen & Son Limited.
Design by Anne Winslow.

This is a work of fiction. While, as in all fiction, the literary perceptions and insights are based on experience, all names, characters, places, and incidents either are products of the author's imagination or are used fictitiously.

Library of Congress Cataloging-in-Publication Data
Southgate, Martha.
The taste of salt : a novel / by Martha Southgate.—1st ed.
p. cm.
ISBN 978-1-56512-925-2
1. African American families—Fiction. I. Title.
PS3569.O82T37 2011
813'.54—dc23 2011024615

10 9 8 7 6 5 4 3 2

For Ruby,
who always makes herself heard

The cure for anything is salt water—
sweat, tears, or the sea.

—ISAK DINESEN

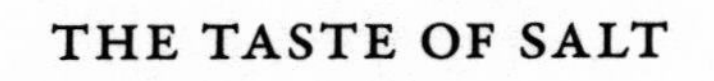

THE TASTE OF SALT

Part One

One

My mother named me after Josephine Baker. I think she was hoping I'd be more artistically inclined. The sort of woman who would sing as she swayed elegantly through the streets of Paris. The sort of woman who would have many men at her feet. The sort of woman men would write songs about. Didn't work out like that, though. I'm kind of tall, like Baker, and medium brown, like her. Can't sing, though. And I don't look too good in a skirt made out of bananas. To my knowledge, no one has ever written a song about me. Everybody calls me Josie—that feels more like my right name to me. My brother is nicknamed Tick, because when he was little, he was such a fast and efficient crawler that my father said he was just like a little watch—ticktock, ticktock. That got shortened to

Tick and it stuck. That's what everybody calls him. His given name is Edmund after the poet Edmund Spenser. That was Daddy's idea, too. He could not get over *The Faerie Queene*. That was one of his favorite books. I've never read it. Looks too complicated to me. I was raised to respect books—the house was full of them. From the time I was little, it was drummed into our heads that books were almost the most important thing in the world, second only to getting a good education. So I've read a lot of fiction's greatest hits—either I had to for school or I felt like I should or Daddy told me to read them. I even enjoyed some of them. But they're not what I'm drawn to. When I read, I want it to be something that I can use. So mostly I read monographs. I read texts. I read science and history. Mostly, I read about what's happening in the ocean. That's enough to fill your mind for a lifetime.

I'm happiest when I'm in the water. Since we've been working at Woods Hole, I don't get as much ocean time as I'd like. It's nothing like Oahu, where we used to live. The water here is murky and green. I dive to keep up my chops, but it can't match the pure blue pleasure of the Pacific. Sometimes I feel a little heartbroken to have left that behind.

My field of study is the behavior of marine mammals, which, let me tell you, is not easy. The ocean doesn't just offer itself up to you. Here's a typical situation: I'm suspended in the bluest water you can imagine, an entire universe flitting past my ears. Something comes up behind me. It's big, it's black, it moves through the water like a dream, no earthly impediments. It's gone. What was it? That's what people don't understand about marine biology—how extraordinary it is that we know what we know (and given all that we suspect is under the sea, believe me, we don't know much). How can you study something that you can't observe at length? How can you track data on a creature you didn't know existed a year ago? How can you truly get to know an environment that you can't live in, that you have to have all kinds of equipment even to spend time in? It's the miracle of my work—of our work—that we are able to know anything at all. The life beneath us is so unfathomable, and we treat it with such disdain. This Woods Hole job is a good one—I couldn't say no, and neither could my husband, Daniel. They offered us both these amazing fellowships, and this *is* Daniel's hometown. But how I miss the warm silence of that part of the Pacific, the things that would surprise me when they swam past my waiting shoulder.

THE WAY I GOT into this work was through my love of the water. I've always known it was where I belonged.

Given that I was born and raised in Cleveland, Ohio, home of one of the least inspiring of the not all that interesting Great Lakes, I've had to work pretty hard to get to where I belong. But I did it. Right after college, my Stanford marine biology degree in hand, I got an unpaid internship at the Shedd Aquarium in Chicago working with the marine mammals. I worked in a Starbucks at night and ate a lot of ramen noodles for those five months but I was the happiest I'd ever been. It was a lot of hauling heavy objects around, a lot of cleaning up, and a lot of tank maintenance, but I got to work with the dolphins sometimes and touch their smooth gray skin. They felt like heaven to me. And then, the miracle: When my twenty weeks were up, one of the full-time animal trainers quit and they asked me to stay on. This job allowed me to get to know the dolphins—their personalities, their quirks, everything about them. I loved them. I really did, almost like the way you'd love a person. It was easier to love them than to love a person.

The Shedd is spectacular. It was built in 1929. The ceiling is like that of a cathedral but it's covered with images of sea life instead of Jesus: simple, earnest paintings of starfish and turtles and whales. There are seashells in bas-relief and pillars everywhere; the whole building has that templelike grandeur that public buildings of that era have. Every day

I walked in looking up over my head, open-mouthed, like a little kid.

The greatest thing about the job was getting to be in the water nearly every day. My favorite part was after I had all my dive equipment on. Rolling in backward and letting the water close over my head. The air coming into me from the oxygen tank on my back so that I was buoyed up and breathing even though there was water all around me. I would cut through it and the fish would swim up and hover around me like jewel-colored birds or butterflies over a field. I love breathing underwater but still being safe, held, protected. I love the weightlessness. I never feel that the rest of the time. Life weighs a ton. That's why I love the water. Nothing weighs anything there.

ALL THE OTHER WOMEN who had the gig were white, and they only had to snatch their hair back into messy ponytails before they dived. I had cornrows at the time; I hadn't yet seen that I had to cut off all my hair and let my head be free. It took me a year to realize it and to get up the nerve to deal with my mother's disapproval. But I finally did. After my first trip to the barbershop, I never looked back. I looked like a sculpture, a beautifully shaped piece of wood. I started to wear big earrings all the time when I wasn't diving—inexpensive silver hoops and flashy teenage-girl sparklers. Now I buy earrings at this shopping-mall chain where I'm usually at least ten years older than anyone else in there. I cut my hair myself once a week with clippers. Sometimes I run my hand over the short, assertive bristles up there and it makes a little shiver go down my legs. I'm never growing it back. Never.

NOT TOO MANY BLACK people work at Woods Hole (the official name is Woods Hole Oceanographic Institution, but no one calls it that). There are some black interns and postdocs, but I am the only black senior scientist there. It's always like that. Black scientists, particularly marine biologists, are very rare.

A lot of black people raised the way I was—in cities, which is most of us—don't like the water. Or perhaps I should say, they never find out whether they'd like it or not. Why? A million reasons dating back a hundred years: hair, money, time, lack of opportunity. It's a shame. I can't imagine what my life would be like if I'd never been given the chance to know the water. Thank God, my mother was different, though she didn't swim herself. We were off to the Y at a young age—but all she ever did at the pebbly freshwater beach of Lake Erie was worry that her hair was going back or getting blown around too much. And my father? He wore oxfords to the beach; we have photographic evidence. In the only picture we have of him on such a trip, his head is lowered and he is scowling at the sand. Not long after that photograph was taken, he stopped going at all. "Don't know what you see in it, Josie," he said. "Sand gets all up under your toenails and in your socks. Takes a week or two to get out, gets all over everything. Plus it's too damn hot. You can have it."

Tick never really got why I loved the water so much either. But he would always go with me. He went down to Lake Erie near our house with me almost whenever I wanted. He'd sift the rocks through his fingers and watch me gather up samples by the shoreline (I've done that since I was about eight—I used one of those dime-store buckets until my mother finally got me a proper collection set). After I got to be a really good swimmer and I was old enough to drive, he'd go out to the beach at Edgewater or sometimes even way out to Mentor Headlands with me, too. But he never wanted to spend the kind of time in the water that I did. He went because he loved me.

DANIEL, MY HUSBAND, IS white. I don't know why I announce it except that it's the first thing you notice, especially around here, the two of us. People don't disapprove but they do notice. Well, here's the other reason I say it—because I notice it myself. I've been with other white guys. Not that many black guys, to tell the truth. Just one, in grad school. It didn't work out for a lot of reasons. But sometimes I wonder what it would have been like to make a life with someone who looked more like me, maybe had lived more like me. I know race isn't the way to make these decisions. But in my secret heart, sometimes, I just wish Daniel knew certain things, certain sounds, certain feelings, in a way that he just can't.

Unlike most of our colleagues, we actually live in Woods Hole. Having property is part of what made us decide to come. Daniel's mother died a few years ago and left him the house. His father was already gone—he died in a boating accident when Daniel was ten. The house needed a lot of work but is now worth quite a bit—when they were building the institute in the 1930s, land was fifty cents an acre. Daniel's parents didn't get it for that cheap—but it was cheap. Anyway, those days are long gone. For most of us scientists, who are hustling for grants when we aren't working on studies and who never get paid that well, this town is way out of reach. Many of my colleagues live in North Falmouth, about twenty miles away.

Anyway, Daniel. He is kind, precise, and quiet. I was drawn to those things about him. I try to be precise but it doesn't come naturally. He's a couple of years older than I am, an ichthyologist. He loves sorting species, classifying them. Me, I'm pleased to see a really rare specimen of something, but I'm not as moved by the idea of collecting.

Daniel's voice softens when he says fish names. Parrotfish. Tarpon. Gar. Sometimes I think I married him because his voice softened in the same way when he said my name. Josie. Squirrelfish. Blue tang. He came along when I'd pretty much given up on men as a gender. I mean, they are the ones I prefer sexually—in college I was with women a few times, but it wasn't for me—but I found them impossible in every other way. I couldn't get them, their behaviors.

When Daniel came along, I was dating a bartender who enjoyed his wares a bit too much—our relationship was on its last, unsteady legs. I don't even quite know how I got involved with a guy like that. He was good in bed; he had the kind of authority that you sometimes find in men who don't think too much. That can keep you going for a while. But not forever. Daniel came along, same field, same smarts, those kind blue eyes that could not stop gazing at me. What could I say? What could I do? I went with him. I loved him. I mean, I love him.

WE DON'T HAVE KIDS. I'm thirty-six, so I know time is running out. I don't feel that frantic urgency that a lot of women do, though. I've never felt like my femaleness is tied up in whether or not I have offspring. To tell the truth, I'm not entirely sure that I want to have kids. Wait. The truth. The truth is, I know I don't want to. Daniel wants them. I don't. When we got married, I honestly thought I'd end up coming around. But I never did. Kids make me nervous. I'm afraid having kids would keep me from the water; I've never had the vision of a brown-skinned, perpetually tanned little fish baby that Daniel talks so wistfully about. I've blamed my unwillingness to pursue infertility treatments on the expense (which we really couldn't afford) and philosophical objections to the artificial manipulation of fertility, but that isn't really it. I'm afraid that I don't have enough to give, that I can't love a baby the way it needs to be loved. Sometimes I'm not even sure I have enough to give Daniel.

I wouldn't know what to say to a child really. How to raise it properly. How to tell it what life is really like. I think about that a lot. Being married, for example. They don't tell you how that's going to feel when you sign up for this deal. You think (well, you're supposed to think), "This is the one. All my troubles are over." That's what all the songs say, the Bible, your mother, your father. Everything points toward a permanent pairing—even though they so rarely work out. To tell the truth, permanent pairings are unnatural—as a biologist, I know that. "You're the one." "You're all I need to get by." "Together forever." It's all in there, that belief that if you find the right person and love them properly, you will never open your heart again. But I'm not sure that's true. How would I explain that to a kid? My mother wouldn't get it. I don't think she's touched a man, or been touched, since my father left—since she put him out—when I was seventeen. I don't know if she really still loves him. It's just that she can't conceive of there being someone else. I can.

THERE'S THIS HOLLOW place in me—this place that needs to be alone, this place that vibrates and can't sit still. My work requires me to be still; but sometimes, in my heart, I feel that toe impatiently tapping, waiting for the other shoe to drop, lonely, scared. I don't know how to explain that to anyone. I'm not sure how to explain it to myself.

I've been like this for as long as I can remember. Sure that it's never going to work out. Sure that it's all my fault. What is, you ask? Everything. Everything that's ever gone wrong in my life or the life of anyone I've loved. A therapist would say that's standard issue for someone who grew up like I did—classic adult-child-of-an-alcoholic stuff (yeah, I know the lingo). But so what? Given that, what the fuck am

I supposed to do? I have to go on from where I am. That's why I don't look back. That's why I put it all behind me, put them all behind me, my family. They live in Cleveland. They don't understand about the ocean. And that means they don't understand about me.

Two

I turn Mom's car into the curving driveway of Riverrun, my brother's latest rehab. There has been one before this. Pray God there are no more after. He's got (well, I think he's still got) a great job, working as a trainer for the Cavaliers. Their employee assistance program paid for this stint. That's a change: Last time Tick was in here, about three years ago, my parents had to hustle it up from insurance and savings, which was more than a notion. I will never forget the look on my mother's face after she brought him home that time. I came home to help and was willing to go with her when she went to get him but she told me she felt better going alone. Afterward, it was obvious that it had torn her heart out, even though his homecoming was supposed to be the hopeful, joyous part. I think she felt that having had a son in rehab was kind of like having had a son in prison. The shame of it. That's what made me agree to come get him this time, as much as I hate being home. Sparing her that moment of seeing him coming out of rehab—especially for the second time? How could I let her go through that again? Besides, I owed it to Tick. We owed each other.

At Riverrun—which is not far from Dean, the prep school where Tick and I were scholarship kids—the grounds gleam with an effortful calm and cheer. There are a lot of flowers, impatiens and other sturdy breeds that grow well without much care. I think the gardeners are trying to combat the disappearance of hope that brings you to a place like this. The sky is silvery and the air smells of leaves—it looks as though it is going to rain soon. There are a few people out on benches by the entrance, all nervously chain-smoking. I used to smoke but I never smoked with that much intensity, like I'd die if one second passed without a cig in my hand. The patients are all different races but have the same grayish pallor, like they don't get outside much. Like they don't even trust outside much. I feel bizarrely sun-soaked and muscular and fit next to them. I lean on the glass door to enter the building.

Tick is sitting alone on a bench by the front office, a small green duffel bag at his feet. His dark, once handsome face is hollowed out around the cheeks and eyes. My baby brother. He looks so old. I almost don't recognize him.

He knows me, though. He hops up from the bench, and when he smiles, there's a ghost of the old Tick who always used to bust into my room without knocking. "Josie, hey, Josie. Thanks for coming to get me."

"What am I supposed to do, leave you here for good?"

"Well, I knew you wouldn't, but you know. . . . It's nice to see you, that's all." He pauses. "I don't think Mom could have stood picking me up."

"Well, what'd you expect?" I say.

He looks at me, his eyes gone to rock. "Do you really need to start in right away with that shit?"

His voice is angry and defensive, the same tone of voice that kept denying that there was a problem even as you could smell it on him, see it on him. The same voice I ran away from, no matter what it cost me. Or him.

But wait, here's a difference. The tirade doesn't continue. The bluster vanishes quickly and his eyes turn sad. "Josie, I'm sorry." He sighs the saddest sigh in the world. "I've got so much to be sorry for. I know that now. I just . . . sometimes old habits are the ones you go to first, you know?"

I look at him for a minute. Then I hug him. He's so thin that I can feel his bones shifting under my arms. "I know. I know." I push away from him for a minute. "Who do I need to see to get you sprung from this joint?" He tells me and I turn and go into the office.

Riverrun is clearly a place that is intended to help people start finding their way out of the darkness, but even so, it has the greenish paint and fluorescent lighting that seems to be endemic to the kind of places where you either get well or die. I think there's a special factory where they manufacture the paint for these sorts of places. A paint factory like the one in Ellison's *Invisible Man* (when I was fifteen, my father came out of his fog long enough to insist that I read that book; the sequence with the paint factory was indelible). I imagine the place where they make these paints is difficult and cold and hopeless like the most battered parts of the former Soviet Union or parts of Detroit or East St. Louis. They pour a little of that despair into every can of paint. I sit down.

There is a drug counselor behind the desk. She looks to be in her forties, a bit older than me. You know how they say that some folks look like they've seen it all? Well, you could tell with one look at her that she'd seen it all, and done most of it, walked away from what hurt her, and was just going to let you have your say. Her earrings are those big gold doorknockers that aren't in style anymore, but on her they look good. She is solid, but not fat. She has a generous smile. The name on her tag is Lakeisha James.

"Ms. James?"

"Yes?"

"I'm Josie Henderson, Edmund Henderson's sister?"

She looks confused. "Edmund? Oh, you mean Tick. And please call me Lakeisha."

I smile a little—he never goes by his right name anywhere. "Yeah, Tick. I'm ready to take him home. Is there anything I need to do?"

"Just fill these papers out, honey. I think Tick's ready to go home. Does he have somewhere to stay?"

"Well . . . he lost almost everything, you know, before he got here. His job, his apartment, all that. But my mother is ready to take him in and help him get on his feet again. And his job said they'd give him one more chance. I . . . I'm here now but I don't live here anymore. I live up in Massachusetts."

She looks at me noncommittally. "Is your mother up to supporting him?"

"Yes, I think she is. She loves him very much."

"She's in good health?"

"Pretty good. Mom's a real go-getter."

"And I understand from Tick that your father has a history of alcoholism, too?"

A click inside. "Yes. Yes, he does. He's sober now, though."

"That's good. How long has that been?"

"I don't talk to him often." Her cool gaze doesn't change but my face gets hot anyway. "My mother has had some contact with him. He slipped up once but he's been sober for about ten years now."

"Sounds like he's over the hump. As much as you ever get over it, anyway—one day at a time," she said, with a shake of her head and a slight smile. "Do you attend Al-Anon meetings?"

"No. I went to a few when I was in college, but I didn't find them that helpful." She looks as though she wants me to say more. I don't know what else to say. The main thing I felt in those meetings was an intense desire to leave. People sat on folding chairs in a circle and told their stories of car crashes and lost homes and vomiting, and I'd think, "Well, my father didn't do any of that. What am I doing here?" After about five times, I stopped going. I hated the slogans—One Day at a Time, Keep the Focus on Yourself—and the way they made you feel like their way was the only way. I hated the folding chairs and the bad coffee. I hated that I was the only college student there, the only scientist, the only dark one. I stood out too much. And I'm not the drunk anyway—why do I have to go to the stupid meetings? I know meetings are great for some people. I'm just not one of them. I mean, in the end we're all on our own anyway, right?

"Well, I'm sorry to hear that. Most of our families find them very useful. But to each his own. Is your father available to help your mother?"

"I think so. I'm not on the best terms with him, but I think they've been talking about how to handle things." I take a deep breath. "They separated when I was seventeen—he got sober after that." I hope she drops this line of questioning.

She nods and grants my wish. "Well, Tick has a tough road ahead. You know this, right?"

"I've heard."

She laughs, then says, "How come your mother isn't here?"

"Why isn't my mother here?"

"You heard me."

"She wanted me to. Tick and I are very close. We were, anyway. My mother thought it would be better if he saw me first."

"But you're leaving town."

A note of steel comes into my voice. "Yes. I'm married. I haven't lived here in more than ten years. I have work I have to get back to." She keeps looking at me with unnerving steadiness, so I keep babbling. "I can't stay. I can't stay."

Finally, she breaks her gaze. "Fine. But I hope you're prepared to support your mother. It's up to Tick to get to meetings and keep himself straight. He might need some help with that. If your mother couldn't bring herself to come here—are you sure she's prepared to give that help?" She hesitates. "Are you sure he hasn't hurt her too much?"

Hasn't hurt her too much. I sit back in the chair for a minute. I remember the day Mom told me that she needed me to come home and help her get Tick out of rehab. That day, my office door was closed and there was a lightning storm outside. The wind sounded like it was crying. I clutched the phone—I could imagine my mother's face even though I couldn't see it. I'd talked to her fairly often over the months that she slowly stopped being able to deny what was happening again with Tick. The last time I saw her, about a month before he went into rehab this time, her eyes were sunk back in her head as though she'd been alive for a thousand terrible years and would be alive for a thousand terrible more. "Josie, it's like he lost his mind. I swear. I've been talking to your father a little bit but it's too hard for me to talk to him much. There's too much water under the bridge. He understands and I think he really has changed, but . . ." Her voice thickened and she had to stop talking. I was holding the telephone receiver so hard that my hand hurt. "I went by Tick's apartment the other day.

The landlord let me in. He knows there's a problem. Josie, it was so filthy—bottles everywhere. I can't . . . an animal wouldn't live the way your brother lives. It's breaking my heart. It's breaking your father's heart. We don't know what to do. I can't believe that we're back here." And I heard in her voice that she'd never meant anything more literally in her life. Her heart was in pieces in her chest, cutting her flesh to ribbons. She didn't know what to do about anything anymore.

Not long after this conversation, he totaled his car on Fifty-fifth and Euclid. Went right up on the sidewalk, knocked over a streetlight. When they picked him up, he couldn't even say the alphabet properly. He went into rehab after that. I helped with the paperwork, but I spoke to him only once while he was there. He wasn't allowed to make too many calls, and when we did talk, he sounded as though he was at the bottom of a well. I couldn't stand it. I know, I know I abandoned him when he needed me. I know that's wrong. But I couldn't stand the aching, hollow sound of his voice.

I think that's why I came home without a fuss when Mom asked me to. I knew that I hadn't been there for the hard part before and I wasn't going to be there for the hard part to come. I could do this little bit of driving. That I could do.

This all goes through my mind rapidly as I sit there. I can't say any of it to Lakeisha James. So I just say this. I say, "We'll manage. We all love Tick very much."

She sighs. "I'm sure you do," she says. I can see her deciding that she isn't getting anything else out of me. She stacks up some papers and shows me where to sign, where Tick already signed. And then it's time to get him and go.

TICK IS SITTING WITH his feet angled toward each other, the way he always did when he was a kid. He looks like he wants a cigarette, his fingers twisting nervously around each other. He looks like he's afraid they won't let him go. Lakeisha smiles broadly and hugs him, saying, "You make those meetings now, you hear?" And Tick nods and she rubs the back of his head like you would a little boy. I stand awkwardly to the side.

After another hug, he is released. He picks up his cheap bag and grins at me. "Let's get out of here," he says. So we do.

"Feels funny being back out here again, huh, Tick?" I say as we pull out of the driveway.

He bristles a bit. "What, that place? I ain't never been there before."

I suck my teeth. "Dag, Tick, I know that. I mean back out by Dean."

"Oh. School. Yeah." He smiles a little. "Actually, I didn't

think about that too much. But yeah. It is weird to be back out here. Especially when you think about why I was out here. He twists toward me away from the side window he's been looking out of. "You mind if I have a cig? I'll open the window."

"Go ahead." I wish he wouldn't smoke in the car—it makes me want a cigarette, too. But I have to grant him this—it's the one addiction he's got left. We hope anyway. I stare straight ahead as he lights up.

Tick reaches out to turn on the radio. I set it to the oldies station on the drive out so the Isley Brothers ease out of the speakers—I don't know why I love all that old stuff. But I do. I laugh. "Remember when I was little and I used to think that everybody on the radio was down there at the station, waiting to go on? I couldn't believe it when Mom told me it was records. You could've knocked me over with a feather."

Tick laughs. "Yeah, I remember. You never was too good at thinking stuff like that through."

"Stuff like that, yeah. I did okay with other stuff though," I say. Tick takes a long drag and looks at me. "What do you mean by that?"

"Nothing. I don't know. I just mean in school and all."

Tick sits straight up. "Damn, Josie, I ain't been out that damn place an hour and you already steady telling me what's wrong with me. I did the best I could. Shit, I know I fucked up." He sighs. "Been steady fucking up. But I'm trying to stop. Always had you as the perfect example in front of me. That didn't help." It's funny listening to him talk—his years with the Cavs have made his voice more . . . well . . . black. More slangy, less grammatical, more like the players—who, let's face it, are mostly young, unpolished black men. You can't hang around an NBA team and not talk the talk. I wonder what Daddy would think about that—he never liked us to sound too "street." I like listening to Tick. I never hear truly urban, black voices anymore. I don't sound like him—in fact, a lot of other kids were only too happy to ask me "How come you talk so white?" for much of my childhood.

I slide the car into the flow of traffic in front of us. "So it's my fault."

"No . . . damn, Josie, no. That ain't what I'm saying. I just had a lot of time to think in there, you know. I been thinking a lot."

I have the feeling that whatever I say will be wrong. So I don't say anything. Tick smokes and looks out the window but then—we're saved by Prince. The song on the radio changes to "Purple Rain," a musical peace offering. I seize on it. "Oh, man Tick, remember when we saw him in concert? That was so amazing."

He grins, "I think you were more amazed than I was."

I change lanes, feeling a little embarrassed for some reason. "I guess I was. Did you know that for weeks after that concert me and Deena used to sit on the porch with that little radio of mine writing down every time they played this?"

"Is that what y'all was doing? For real? I never knew why you two sat out there like that all that time." He laughs. "Thought you were watching the cars go by. Or the fireflies once it got dark. I never could figure it out."

"Yeah, well, you were too busy hanging out in old McNeil's lot, getting into trouble." McNeil's lot is a large overgrown tract of land behind our block that, for some reason, no one had ever bought and developed. You could get in there easily by going around the corner from our house. It was best known for kids hanging out there and committing nefarious acts—sometimes childish, sometimes not.

"Mmf." He pauses and takes a long drag. "You know they mowed that all down now and put a big fence around it. It ain't nothing but a big vacant lot now. Nobody hangs out there anymore."

"Really?"

"Yeah. It's a shame." Another long pause. "A lotta things changed since you left, Josie. A lotta things."

I let that hang in the air. It's not like I didn't know

that. I decide to go ahead and say what I've been thinking about—the hardest question. "You gonna stay clean this time, Tick?"

He flicks his cigarette out the window and rubs his hands across his pants legs. He looks out the window. "Sure gonna try. I know I owe that to everybody. To try."

He's like a stone around my neck, around all our necks. Is he really ready to set us free? Neither of us says another word the rest of the way home. "Purple Rain" ends and the Brothers Johnson's "Strawberry Letter 23" comes on. We might be kids again, sitting silently together, our thoughts washing over us like waves.

When we pull up to the house, Mom is sitting out front. She's gained weight recently, even though she knows better—she's a cardiac care nurse. Her hair is gray, straightened, and short. It's beautifully cut—she's more careful about that kind of thing since she got heavier. Her half-glasses sit on the end of her nose and she's wearing jeans and a tunic and sneakers. She looks like herself. Tired and worn but the self I've always known. The big surprise is that Daddy is sitting next to her. Their legs are almost touching and they're both looking straight ahead. I haven't seen my father in nearly a year—it's been that long since I'd come home to visit. He looks good. His skin is even and clear and he's lost weight. His hair, which has thinned very little, is gray and close-cropped and he's wearing jeans and a polo shirt. Even though I knew that they've become friendlier as time's gone by and he's stayed sober, there's also this voice in me that's still about sixteen. It's yelling: *You threw him out. How can you let him back into your life? If you threw him out, that's that.* They look like statues together there, quiet, dark, and still. They don't stand up the minute we pull into the driveway. It takes a moment for them to pull themselves together to look really happy to see me driving their son, my brother, home. "Tick, did you know Daddy was going to be here?" I ask. I hate the way my voice is shaking.

He stubs his cigarette out. "Yeah, Mom told me. My group they thought it might be good for me to see him. And I don't know. I said all right."

Our parents stand up and come toward us. Tick gives me one last nervous look and climbs out of the car. He moves toward the porch and drops his bag on the ground. "Mom?" He takes an uncertain step toward her.

Her face shatters. I don't know any other way to describe it. All that loss and anger and that she loves him anyway—it is all in her sorrowing face. She can't ever stop loving him, even if it might make her life easier. Never. Does she feel that way about me? I suppose so. But I've never been as much trouble—nor am I as charming—so I've never been in the spotlight the way Tick has. She steps toward Tick with her arms open and it is as though I have never existed at all. My father grimaces uncomfortably—maybe, like me, he sees that she has never loved him the way she loves the man in front of her, the one she'd given birth to, the one they'd raised. Or maybe he is thinking of his part in all the pain my mother has borne.

Tick and my mother hold each other for a long time, making little noises, almost like lovers. I stare at the maple tree on the front lawn. My father stands with his hands limp at his sides. It is so quiet you can hear the wind move through the leaves.

They break their embrace, my mother wiping at her cheeks like an embarrassed child, Tick standing so close that their shoulders touch. A big black Escalade drives by, booming "Dirt Off Your Shoulder." My father says, "Let's go in." He and I lead the way. He walks ahead of me but I can still see his face in my mind. He looks older and more relaxed and handsome than he did when I was young; each year he spends sober seems to make time itself sit more easily on him. He seems settled into his soul, if you believe in that kind of thing—I'm not sure I do. He says hello but he doesn't try to touch me. I think he wants to. But he doesn't.

We sit in the living room and I suddenly wish Daniel was with me. He offered to come but I told him he didn't have to—that it was too expensive and that it would be easier if he didn't. But that's not true. He has an ease with my family that I don't. That's pathetic, I know, but that's how it is. Maybe he's more relaxed because they are not his blood kin. He didn't live with them and see my father's quiet disappearance into a beer can or watch Tick start to disappear after him. He just takes them the way he finds them now. Back when we got married, I was still so angry with Daddy that I wasn't going to invite him to our wedding, but Daniel insisted. We fought over it. I finally gave in when we were arguing about it (again) and his eyes actually welled up. He said, "You will be sorry for the rest of your life if you don't invite him to your wedding, Josie. I know it. My father's dead. He can't be with us, and I'm telling you . . . you don't want to throw away the chance to have him there. I know he's hurt you, but he should be there, even if you can't stand to talk to him." He was almost crying about it and I wasn't. That made me think that perhaps I should soften my stance. And you know what? He was right. Sometimes I think that's why I married Daniel—to soften my stance. He would have known what to say as Tick fidgeted in front of the mantelpiece and my father sat down in the same chair that he always sat in, even though it hasn't been his living room for many years. My mother and I sit on the edge of the sofa. I wish I could leave. But of course I can't.

"So I've got the basement fixed up for you, Tick," my

mother volunteers. "I know you won't be there long. Just until you get back on your feet."

Tick puts down the figurine that he has been awkwardly fiddling with on the mantelpiece. "Thanks, Ma. I appreciate that."

"And son, I've got a list of AA meetings. I'm sure they gave you one but it's good to have one on you." This from my father. He extends a printed pocket-size booklet toward Tick.

Tick looks right through him. I can see that he wants that list but, at the same time, he doesn't want Daddy to be the one he takes it from. After a frozen moment, he reaches out and takes it. My father nods and then stands up. "I guess I better be getting on. Tick, you be in touch when you need to, all right?" He stands and walks to him, puts a hand squarely on his back and lets it rest there for a few moments. Tick turns his eyes from the mantel after a minute and looks at him, but he doesn't offer an embrace. Daddy nods once more and then steps toward me. I stand up and he puts his arms around me. Like an awkward teenager, I stand there with my arms hanging straight down my sides. He pushes me away from him and looks into my eyes but doesn't speak. He sighs and turns to my mother, saying, "So, Sarah—we'll talk?"

"Yes, Ray. We will." She gives him a real hug and walks

him to the door. Tick and I stare after them, united in bafflement and anxiety, like we used to be. Not like two people in their thirties. More like a couple of kids.

My mother comes back. "Well, I'd better get dinner started," she says, her voice twinkling like a television mother's. And with that, she goes off to the kitchen. Tick looks at me for a long moment. "Damn," he says, "ain't that something. With Daddy, I mean?"

"It's something, all right. He looks good, huh?"

Tick sits down in Daddy's chair and looks out the window. "I guess."

"He might be able to help you, you know. He's . . . well . . . he's been there, right?"

Tick looked away from me, through me, his eyes hard. "No one has been where I've been. No one." After all the phone calls and the worry and the agony, when he says that, that is the most frightened I've been.

Three

I'm a scientist. I like to get to the bottom of things, to state the working hypothesis quickly. Narrative is not my specialty. But when I stop to think about it, in some ways, telling a story is like science. Trying to understand how a system works, what makes it function or not function, that's part of what a story does. Nothing is unrelated to the things that came before it. It's true of evolution and it's true of a family. I am, in part, the sum of all who came before me, my parents and brother, their parents and siblings, and on and on, back onto the slave ships and then back farther, back to Ghana and the slave castles at Elmina and to wherever my ancestors were before that.

So right now I'm going to leave the scene with my brother and my parents. Indulge me as I tell the story of a family, the story of my family. I will invite in other voices, because one thing I've learned in science is that the first truth you see is rarely the whole truth. I will hypothesize and extrapolate, if you will. I will even imagine scenes I did not witness, speak the thoughts of other people. Theories can't be formed and understanding can't be reached without hypothesis, extrapolation, and though we in the biz don't like to admit it, imagination. So I'll start in 1969, five years before I was born. That year, my father, Ray Henderson, met my mother, Sarah Jenkins. Back then, Cleveland was only beginning its long, slow decline. Despite the riots in Hough in 1966 and King's death just a couple of years later, there was still plenty of industrial work available right in the city. My father worked at the Coit Road GM plant for nearly twenty years. Do you know how many car doors he must have attached in that amount of time? The mind reels. And drinking steadily much of the time. He never missed a day of work either. I don't know how he did it. Any more than I knew how to get him to stop.

In 1969, long before he could even have dreamed how things would go in his life, he was a tall, good-looking twenty-nine-year-old with money in his pocket and a smooth, sweet way of whistling.

Back then, a man could always find work if he was

willing. There was money to be made in Cleveland, and plenty of places to spend it. East 105th Street glowed like the Las Vegas strip. Every Saturday night, there'd be folks pimpwalking up and down the street, going from club to club. In the fifties, it was Muddy Waters and Coltrane and all the big names. Later, Motown moved in—Smokey Robinson and the Miracles and the Supremes and God only knows who else. But you can bet it was somebody good. They all came through Cleveland. If you walk down 105th now, the street is nearly a ghost town in the few places where it isn't covered by the hulking red-brown buildings of the Cleveland Clinic. 105th Street near Euclid is a series of shabby attempts at strip malls and a dazzling number of fast-food places and boarded-up businesses and factories. Head further downtown into the East Sixties and Seventies and the scene is much the same.

But when Ray met Sarah at Leo's Casino on East Seventy-ninth in 1969, this was all in the future. Aretha Franklin was coming through that night. The air was alive, sparkling. Ray was nursing a beer when my mother came in. Sarah was tiny and delicate-boned—she looked like music and sunshine. She had big brown eyes and the prettiest smile he'd ever seen. She came in with a girlfriend, but the girlfriend didn't make much of an impression on Ray. The women sat down at the bar, just a stool away from him, and ordered some girly kind of drinks. Something pink with a silly name. Sarah sat there like a little bird, looking at everything that was going on around her, so interested. Ray found himself looking at her mouth as she sipped at her drink. After a few minutes he got up and walked over to them.

"Hello, ladies," he said. The friend made a little pout and looked away, but Sarah looked up and looked Ray right in the eye. "Hello," she said.

"What brings you here tonight?"

"We love Aretha Franklin." This was from the friend, who immediately established herself as the bossy one. Ray played along—he could wait. And if they were friends, no sense alienating the one when you wanted to get to the other.

"Oh, yeah, that sister is all right. Y'all from down south?"

"No sir," said the friend. "We both come from Chicago. We came here to go to school. We've been here about two months. We go to the Bolton nursing school—in that new building over at Case Western."

Nursing school? An educated woman? A pretty black woman like her knows enough about having a good time to come out and see Aretha *and* is in nursing school? Ray felt as though he must have done something right that day to meet someone like her. He thought of his small, book-cluttered room and how he didn't dare tell anyone he worked with about how much he loved to read—they found out later, but not then. "What you wanna know all that white-boy stuff for?" they would ask. And laugh. He couldn't explain it to them. That it wasn't "white boy" stuff. It was human stuff. That's why he loved it so: because he just felt human when he read it. Maybe a college girl would appreciate that. No one from back home in Alabama did—not that he ever even talked to them anymore. There was no one he could share it with. He looked at the friend again and said, "Well, can you ladies tell me your names before I buy us all another round?"

The friend, who seemed to feel that she should do all the talking, said, "Thanks. My name's Elizabeth and this here is Sarah." Sarah turned her gaze on Ray and smiled, and that was it. He was gone. Choirs of angels and all the rest. He said to both of them but mostly looking at Sarah, "Well, it's nice to meet you." But Elizabeth might as well have been a post, a tree, a rock. He managed to take a step closer to Sarah and she said, her voice music only he could hear, "Nice to meet you, too."

So that was it. They talked, they drank, they listened to Aretha (who rocked the house; she tore up "I Say a Little Prayer" that night). He somehow managed to maneuver himself so that he was standing next to Sarah. He could smell her. Back home, before he came up north, it was mostly work and sweat, work and sweat. Didn't have time to notice much else. But sometimes, just for a minute at the end of the day, the air would clear and he could forget about the work for a minute and it would smell sweet, the warmed earth all around him, sometimes the sound of a bird. She smelled like that. Sitting next to her gave him that same feeling of peace. Her hair was pressed with a hot comb, and it smelled a little burned and a little like Ultra Sheen, but he could still smell the sweet earth underneath. When it was time for the girls to leave, she slipped her number into his hand when Elizabeth wasn't looking, before he could even ask. He didn't know why she did it like Elizabeth wouldn't approve. But he liked that, too. That she would give her number to a man in a bar, something a proper girl would never do. He liked that.

HE DIDN'T WAIT TOO long to call her. He kept thinking about that smile, how it lifted him up. He kept thinking about her mouth. Her hands looked strong, like she used them a lot, taking care of people. She looked like a person who took good care. She had long, elegant fingers and smooth, perfectly shaped nails. He didn't usually notice a woman's nails but he noticed hers. Maybe because they made such a beautiful, light contrast to her dark skin.

Skin he could imagine pressing his lips to. He was thinking about that as he called her, as they talked, as she agreed to have dinner with him.

SHE WAS WEARING a light pink dress with a full skirt. It set off her skin beautifully, making it look warm and velvety. The sight of her struck him dumb—it seemed he was being offered everything he'd ever wanted. "Well?" she said, hands on hips, mock-annoyed, when he didn't even say hello or stick out his hand to shake or anything.

"You look so beautiful."

She laughed. "Now, that's what a woman likes to hear in the first ten minutes of a date." She took his hand, unself-consciously. "Come on."

So that's how it started. They went out to a steak house not far from where they'd met. They talked and talked. Neither of them could believe how easy it was to talk to each other. Neither of them were virgins. But finding someone you could share your mind with wasn't the same as finding someone you could share your body with. Sarah kept laughing, and after a while, would punctuate what she said with a light touch on his shoulder or his arm. Ray kept having this music feeling about her—the same joy he felt when he was in a club or at a concert and everything was perfect, the music was perfect, freeing something inside of him. He took her hand after a little while. He told her about the shotgun shack where he was born, in a town near Mobile that was so small that it wasn't on any maps. About deciding to follow a friend up north to a decent job after his parents died. There was no one left in Alabama for him by that time anyway—he was the last of three and ten years younger than his youngest sister—they were long gone to different cities up north and had left their baby brother behind as surely as they had left behind the red dirt of the South. She listened, fascinated. Then she told her story; it was very different from his. She was the daughter of one of very few black doctors in Chicago—she'd gone to Howard and, after that, decided that she wanted to help people in the same way her father did. He didn't say anything while she told him all this. But his heart shriveled up a little—why would she keep going out with a man who had barely even finished high school? Who was working on an assembly line just to keep body and soul together. He was alone in the world; she had all the warm cushion that family and money could provide. What did she see when she looked at him?

But her gaze never wavered, steady and warm. It wasn't long before he found himself telling her things that he hadn't told anyone. Things that no one else would listen to: About what it was like to read the books he loved, go all over the world in his imagination, and then spend the day on the line at the auto plant, hanging doors on car after car after car. About how he hoped that wouldn't be all he'd ever do, that he'd like maybe to write a book himself. He'd like to tell a story about the people he knew, the way Ralph Ellison had, the way Langston Hughes had. She listened and nodded and smiled. And at the end of the night, they knew there would be other nights.

And there were: dinners and walks and visits back to that club. She sometimes had a glass of wine or a fruity drink but mostly she stuck to club soda. He always had a beer or two but not too many, never too many. And after a few—no, many—nights of talking, there was the night he told her this story. This was the story that made her fall in love with him for good.

Here's what he told her: "I been working at the GM plant since I came up here. When I first come up north, I rented a room so tiny and so filthy that it made me want to cry or punch something whenever I set foot inside of it. I missed the outdoors something awful. So I would walk the streets after work. Didn't know a soul in this city. The library was open late and it was warm. So one night I walked in there. I hadn't been up here more than three months.

"It was pretty empty, close to closing time. The woman behind the counter could have been from down home. That surprised me, seeing her there. But there she sat, big as life.

She was reading herself, just waiting for the last half hour to pass so she could close up, I suppose. She was reading *Invisible Man*. She looked up at me and smiled. 'May I help you, young man?' I didn't know what to say. I didn't even know why I'd come in. I said the first thing that came to mind. 'It's cold out and it's warm in here. What are you reading?'

"She laughed, even though I hadn't said anything funny. She lifted up the book so I could see it better. '*Invisible Man*. It's by Ralph Ellison,' she said.

" 'Who's he?'

"She showed me his author picture. He looked a little like my daddy. I know I must have looked like someone slapped me. 'He's black?' Though I'd been reading a lot, I'd yet to encounter a black writer—hard to believe, I know. But it's the truth.

" 'Yes indeed,' she said, giving me a good long look. To this day, I don't know what she saw there. But instead of chasing me out of the library, she said, 'Wait a minute.' And she went and got another copy of that book off the shelf and gave it to me. Showed me how to get a library card, too. I took that book home that night and started reading. I'll never forget how it began: 'I am an invisible man. No, I am not a spook like those who haunted Edgar Allan Poe; nor am I one of your Hollywood-movie ectoplasms. I am a man of substance, of flesh and bone, fiber and liquids—and

I might even be said to possess a mind. I am invisible, understand, simply because people refuse to see me.' Well, that was that. No going back after I read those words—and all that followed. No going back to the man I was before. I had to go back to the librarian a lot—Miss Scott her name was—and ask her what certain things meant. She helped me. She helped me learn how to use a dictionary and how to think and she helped me find what to read after Ellison and after that and after that. I don't know if I ever thanked her. But I should have. I hope I see her again someday so I can do that.

"The books saved me in the end. Really saved me. Because I was still at a point where I easy could have gone either way. Yeah, I was earning good money at GM but I hustled a little, too. Nothing that was gonna get me killed, just little shady stuff. Some pool hustling, a little run and gunning; I was a lookout for a numbers runner, kept a little extra money in my pocket. And I'll admit it—I kind of liked the guys. But here's what happened in the end:

"It was a clear August night and I was looking out, just like I was supposed to. Folks were coming and going, playing the numbers, playing that foolish hope, just like they always do, just like usual. I was reading *The Faerie Queene*. I'd come that far, can you believe it? You know what that is? It's from the 1500s—it's all what you call Spenserian sonnet form. Edmund Spenser, the guy who wrote it, invented the way he wrote it. Can you imagine? Damn. When I first started it, I couldn't make head or tail of it. But I taught myself enough, with Miss Scott's help, to read something like that. Not only read it, love it. I loved it. I was living inside it, so far away from Cleveland, so far away from the assembly line, so far away from the numbers, so far from the smell of cigarette smoke.

"So I was reading and reading and reading, and gradually, I stopped looking up. I stopped looking out. I was tucked into this little alcove so I could see but not be seen. I had just read these lines,

> Rest is their feast, and all things at their will;
> The noblest mind the best contentment has

when I heard all this noise. I finally looked up. Five white cops were past me and busting through the door—only reason they didn't grab me was that I was off to the side a little. I have never been so fucking scared—pardon my French. If the cops didn't get me, then Bootsy, the numbers guy, sure as hell would if I didn't get out of there that goddamn minute. And I do mean far away. Jesse Owens didn't have nothing on me that night. You ain't never seen a Negro run the way I ran that night. And while I was running, all I kept thinking was, 'I'm done with this. I'm done with this. I'm done with this.' "

The night he told Sarah this story was the first night they ever made love. After he finished this story, she just looked at him. She seemed to have lost her powers of speech. But she put her hand over his. They were silent. After a while she said, "Why don't we go to your apartment?"

Ray's apartment wasn't much, though it was a step up from the nasty little room he rented when he first got to Cleveland. This place had doors and a separate bedroom, at least. They didn't talk much on the way there. But they did hold hands.

Once they were inside, they both looked a little frightened. There was so much feeling between them. Ray wished he'd had one more drink before they came up. (Was that when it started? Was that when?) He had opened the door and let Sarah walk in ahead of him. He shut the door and she turned to him and opened her arms and took him in. He'd never been taken in like that before. She enfolded him absolutely. She gave him every inch of herself and he did the same.

THEY DID WHAT PEOPLE do—nothing special, nothing new. But they took their time. They kept looking at each other and touching each other everywhere. They weren't shy or afraid. *She* wasn't shy or afraid. She showed him what she liked. She showed him what was right. Much, much later, after it was all gone, Ray would sometimes think, "If only I had kept listening to her."

Four

My parents married in 1970, when they were in their late twenties. My mother was finishing up nursing school and Daddy was dreaming of getting off the assembly line. All things seemed possible to them. My mother loved her work and she loved her husband. My father? He loved his wife. He put up with his job. He had to. What else was he going to do? He put his energy into loving her and reading everything he could get his hands on. On the weekends, he tried to write a novel, sitting down at the typewriter Saturday mornings, a cup of coffee in hand. He slid a clean sheet of paper under the platen and rolled it in. Almost instantly, his mind would go blank. He would sit there, staring at the blank page nervously for a little while—then get up to refill his coffee cup or take a walk or something.

Sometimes he wrote a sentence or two. They never sounded very good to him, though. He couldn't imagine how Ralph Ellison had found the will to stick to the ideas and images and story until they came out clear, like raindrops on a gray day.

My mother loved to see him sitting at the keyboard. She believed something beautiful would come out of it someday. She believed that he'd find a way off the assembly line eventually. She wasn't sure how but she was sure that he would. Everybody at his job called him Professor, Prof for short. Both he and Sarah loved that.

Sarah didn't like to admit to herself that she felt a little odd about having married someone who worked on an assembly line. She had been raised to marry a college man—someone from Howard or Hampton. And a small corner of her still wanted that. She knew when he finished that book that he would show everyone what she already knew; he'd show the world how smart he was, how special. She loved that he was trying, that he was willing to try. She loved that he didn't seem to need her to take care of him—in fact, he liked to take care of her. He gave her back rubs and foot rubs, indulgences that she'd never had from anyone. He made her laugh harder than anyone she'd ever known. And he was as bright as the day was long, despite his mind-deadening job. How she loved to watch him sit with a book in the evenings, while she knitted or read something else, the light spilling over his shoulder as he read. She loved how he had made himself. She loved *that* he had made himself. She loved that he had come from nothing and made himself an educated man.

One night, after they had been married for three years and she was heavily pregnant with me, they were sitting and reading, the way they often did. Ray didn't read aloud often, but this evening, he looked up and said to her, "Hey, doll. Listen to this." Then he read these words:

> Wave of sorrow
>
> Do not drown me now.
>
> I see the island
>
> Still ahead somehow.
>
> I see the island
>
> And its sands are fair.
>
> Wave of sorrow
>
> Take me there.

The last words echoed in the room. After a long silence she said, "That's beautiful. Who wrote that?"

Ray smiled. "It's called 'Island.' It's by Langston Hughes. He used to live around here, you know. He went to Central High."

"Yeah?"

"Yeah."

Sarah reached her hand out. "Can I see the book?"

He handed it to her. She read the poem over and over. And in the days to come, she found herself murmuring the words under her breath. She said it to herself so many times that after a few weeks, she knew she'd never forget it, that the poem beat through her blood now. There were times, later on, when those words that Langston and Ray had given her were all she had to hold on to. But the day she learned that poem, a wave of sorrow seemed very far away.

SHE LOVED HER JOB then. She had finished school and was working at Mount Sinai, not far from home. She loved the rhythm of her days. She was a surgical nurse—there weren't too many black women doing that. The black women who did the work she did were just starting to band together—she had been at the first meeting of the National Black Nurses Association, which was founded right downtown. She stayed active in it for a long time, licking stamps and making phone calls. She liked feeling a part of something bigger than herself. She loved the precision of her job—helping, handing the doctor the right instrument at just the right time, getting to know the bloody order that resides in each human. She loved the taking-care part of her job, too—consoling sobbing wives, holding the hand of a frightened stranger. She often felt that she was born to take care of people this way, born to stand by holding someone's hand as they suffered. Maybe that's why she stayed with my father as long as she did.

She quit working just a few weeks before I was born. The different shifts and the constant on-her-feet time just got to be too much—Ray couldn't rub it away after a while. There was no flextime back then, no way to work anything out. If you got pregnant, you left your job. Period.

She decided to quit one Friday night after a ten-hour shift. She sat on the sofa, her feet in Ray's strong hands. He rubbed intently, looking at them, sometimes offering a playful kiss to one of her toes. Suddenly, she started crying.

"Hey, hey, doll, what is it?"

"Ray, I can't keep working like this. I know we need the money and I really love the work. But my back hurts all the time and I come home and just feel like I'm gonna die. The doctor said I might have to stop when I got this far along. I was hoping I'd be different."

He never stopped rubbing during this whole speech. When she wiped her eyes and stopped crying, he said quietly, "We'll be fine. You go on and give your notice. You gotta take care of yourself and the baby."

My mother looked at him with wonder. He rested one of

her feet in his lap and picked up his beer to take a sip. She leaned over to kiss him, hard, not even minding the beeriness. "Thanks."

FIRST ME AND THEN Tick, barely two years apart, into everything. They hadn't meant to have the children so close together. But one night they'd finally gotten me to sleep. They started kissing and just got carried away. Carried away with that night was life as the parents of an only child. I was only eighteen months old when she found out that Tick was coming. Ray tried to put a good face on it when she told him but she knew. She felt the same way. It was just too soon for another baby. They were stretched so thin already.

And Tick was a difficult baby. You wouldn't know it to look at him. He was a perfect brown butterball, dimpled and angelic looking. Until the evening, when the colic came on him and she and Ray would have to take turns walking and walking and walking and walking while Tick screamed himself into a sleep that was more like unconsciousness. It went on for hours. It went on for days into weeks into months. At first she asked her friends about it, but then their fussy babies stopped fussing and they could offer no more counsel. He cried for four hours every night for four months. At first Ray helped her, but then he told her that he was so tired at work that he was afraid of making mistakes that would cost him his job, so then she took over.

Ray was reading less and getting up from the typewriter faster on Saturday mornings, if he sat down at all, and somewhere in Sarah's exhausted mind, out of the corner of her half-asleep, bloodshot eye, she could see that the beer he'd always enjoyed was becoming a little more omnipresent. It crept up so slowly and her life was such a blur of diapering and wiping and walking and strolling and cooking and cleaning that she couldn't be sure. But every now and then she would look at him, and he would be sitting in front of the television, a beer in his hand, and she'd realize that this was happening almost every evening.

This next part is a little weird for me to imagine—what child, even once grown, likes to imagine her parents' most intimate lives? But if I'm going to tell it, I want to tell it all. Some of this I guess at, some of this I put together from hints, clues, asides that my mother shared with me. She was so lonely a lot of the time, especially when I was younger. Sometimes, I was the only person she had, I think. So. Anyway. Here's what I think might have happened:

She didn't know what to do. She still loved him. And he was in the house. He was working and bringing home his paycheck. He didn't hit her. He didn't yell or curse at her or the children. He still spoke to her; he wasn't out in some bar. She didn't know what to think.

One year passed, then two, then three. She got in the habit of going to bed before Ray did. She was so tired, doing all the work to take care of the babies and the house and everything else. He didn't lift a finger—that was another thing that had changed. They used to do chores together and have a good time doing them. He'd do the dishes while she swept or something like that, and they'd joke around. But somehow he had just stopped helping with all that. She didn't have the nerve to ask him about it. It seemed too petty to talk about. He was tired from work. He had to do a lot of overtime now that she wasn't bringing anything in, and with the two kids, it was a lot to ask. It made perfect sense that he would do less around the house. Things had to be divided up somehow. Still, she wished he would notice how hard she was working to keep things nice. How hard she was working to raise good, smart, kind, polite children.

A winter night. She was lying in bed, Tick and me finally asleep. She had her hand on her stomach, under her nightgown. Not as tight as it used to be, but not bad, considering. She was thinking about how he used to touch her. There hadn't been much of that recently either. The time when they had spent hours, days, visiting each other's bodies like favorite countries was long gone.

Much of the time, she didn't even want to be touched. She was often worn out herself. She rarely thought of making love to him anymore. But this night she did. She was still awake when he came in. He sat on the edge of the bed, and it sagged under his weight as he lay down. He was wearing only boxers and a T-shirt. He lay on his back, breathing evenly. He smelled of beer and fatigue. She rolled over toward him and reached for him. And he turned toward her—sweet surprise—and started kissing her. But it wasn't like it used to be. He seemed distracted, like he was kissing her to forget something else that was bothering him. Despite this, she felt herself responding. She didn't want to stop so she moved her head down to kiss his chest and his stomach. She tried—they both did. But nothing happened. Finally, he pulled away from her and rolled over without a word. "Ray?" she said, moving up so he could hear her. "It's all right, Ray. I don't—"

"It's not all right. Nothing is all right, damn it. Why can't you see that, woman?" He hit the mattress in front of him so hard that she could feel it vibrate. She pulled back a little, though she knew in her bones that he would never hit her. "Why can't you see that? Damn it."

She didn't say anything. It seemed that she would never have anything to say again. The room was shrouded in silence. It was very late by the time she finally fell asleep.

THE NEXT DAY, THEY didn't talk about what had happened. Just got up and she fixed him breakfast and he went to work and came home. But this time, without a six-pack. Her heart leapt at the sight of his empty hands. He played with me and Tick while she fixed dinner, another change. He ate an elaborate pretend meal that I fixed for him in my play kitchen (I don't remember this, but I like to think it happened), and he helped Tick build with his LEGOS, his voice low and patient. She was afraid to breathe. But finally, once she got us down to sleep, she went into the living room and sat next to him on the sofa. He didn't look at her. "Ray?"

He still didn't look at her.

"Ray, I'm glad you came home the way you did tonight and played with the kids and all. But will you talk to me?"

He still didn't look at her. He used to gaze at her so hard she thought he was trying to see her soul. He used to gaze at her so hard that she sometimes had to turn her head away; she couldn't stand it. Being loved that much. It made her blush. It made her nervous. It made her so happy. And now he wouldn't look at her at all. She got up and turned off the television and stood in front of him. "Ray, please, please talk to me. I see how you're trying. I don't care, I don't care about what happened last night. I don't think any less of you, but I gotta know that we're in this together. I gotta know that you're still my husband." She paused. "That you still love me."

"I love you, Sarah. I do." He sighed from the very soles of his feet. "But I know I'm not helping you. I know . . ." He paused. "I know that I'm drinking too much. You think I felt like a man after last night? No. No, I know I'm not right. And I'm gonna try to get right and do right by you all. I swear I am. I swear it."

She went to him and embraced him, just like she did the first time they were ever together. She could feel all of him enter into her arms. He picked her up like she was a feather—after having two kids!—and carried her to their room, and they made love and this time it was perfect. It was so so sweet. If she'd known what was to come, she would have treasured it more. She would have held it to her heart like the jewel it was. But she didn't know. How could you know something like that? How could you hold on to something like that? You couldn't.

Five

When I was eight, nine, ten, I was in love with my father. Of course I was. That's what girls do. And despite all the hard times, there are some good days to remember. That's what makes the bad ones harder to accept. I always thought that if I could just do the right thing, if I could just say some magic words I didn't know, that I could make the good days stay, maybe even multiply. That's what people always think. That's what's so hard to let go of.

When I was eight, nine, ten, my world was my block and the few blocks around it. I went to school and sat through reading and perked up at math and came home. I stroked our cat, Purrface, and cleaned out the litter box. I played Barbies with my friend Deena from across the street. I collected leaf samples from our front yard and classified them by size. I rode bikes with Tick. He had learned to ride when he was four by tilting his tricycle over onto two wheels. He used to spend hours—even at that age—falling and getting up, falling and getting up. And then finally he got up and stayed right and sailed all the way to the corner tilted over like a circus clown. My mother and father were sitting out on the porch when he got the hang of it. I don't think I'd ever seen them laugh so hard. And the next day, my father came home from work with a new red two-wheeler for Tick. We barely ever got him off it after that. As long as there wasn't a foot or two of snow on the ground, he was out furiously riding, riding, riding. Like he was chasing something—or something was chasing him. I could never keep up.

CLEVELAND DOESN'T HAVE AN aquarium anymore, but when I was a kid, there was a pretty good-sized one. It was on its last legs during my childhood—it closed in 1986 when I was twelve. But it was there. I don't remember what the outside of the building looked like. It must have been big. I remember only a feeling of size and of coolness and darkness and mystery. It smelled kind of musty but there was a pleasant hum in the air, the sound of all that water being aerated, the shouts of children on field trips and families out together. It was my very favorite place, but I remember the four of us going there only one time, when I was about nine—all my other visits were on school field trips or with the families of friends.

In retrospect, I imagine that my father was on the wagon that time—he would stop drinking periodically for a few weeks, sometimes even a month or two. My mother's step would lighten and the frown lines on her forehead would fade. Tick and I would fight less, afraid of making the magic disappear and the old Dad reappear. But he always did. I could never really believe that it didn't matter how I behaved. That my father's drinking had nothing to do with me.

The trip to the aquarium had a special kind of holiday feeling to it—it was Father's Day and my father, knowing how much I loved the aquarium (Tick liked it there, too, if not as much), said there was nothing he'd like better than to spend the day with us there. In the car on the way over, he was in an ebullient mood, singing bits of old Chuck Berry songs and putting his hand on the back of my mother's neck. She looked young and pretty, the way I imagine she looked when she first met my father. I had a brief unsettling vision that they had a life that had nothing to do with Tick or me, but I couldn't articulate it, so I picked a fight with Tick instead. Nothing was gonna mess up this day, though. Rather than bellowing and scaring us into quiet, as he sometimes did, Daddy looked up into the mirror with a gentle "Come on, y'all. We're almost there" that somehow got under our skin. So we stopped fighting.

The parking lot was already full of happy-looking Sunday families—mothers and fathers and varying numbers of children. Tick and I held hands as we walked through the parking lot. I know brothers and sisters never do stuff like that but that's how close we were then. We were each other's best allies—I thought that would never change. The four of us went in through the dark entrance hall. The first tank we saw was the one with the electric eel.

It was huge and gray, twisting quietly through the water. For all that it was enormous, it didn't look particularly menacing, swimming soundlessly, ceaselessly back and forth. It had a gray muscularity, an *ownership* of the water that I found beautiful.

People were gathering in front of the tank—there was a sign saying that there would be an eel demonstration in ten minutes. What was it going to demonstrate? I thought. It just swam around—what other skills could it have? Tick and I asked Daddy if we could stop and wait to see what happened. After a few minutes, a man in an army-green shirt and khaki pants came out—he was wearing a head mic, like Madonna's. I thought that was cool. He waved to the small crowd and explained that the electric eel fed itself by stunning its prey with up to 650 volts of electricity. He said he had to put on rubber gloves even to reach into the tank, that a shock from the eel could knock him unconscious. The eel eased placidly through the water. I stared, mystified but excited; I could feel Tick breathing beside me. My father's hand was on my shoulder. The keeper dropped some smaller fish into the tank. They swam around briefly and then, one by one, seemed suddenly to fall asleep. The eel inhaled them without ever slowing down its leisurely circuit of the tank. Now the keeper held up a panel of lights with two long clips dangling from it at the end of black cords. He reached into the tank with both hands and lifted the smooth, strong eel out. He laid it on a little platform over the tank. Everyone in front of the tank stood as still as Sunday morning. He put the clips onto the eel. At first flickering, then all at once, the panel of lights turned on. Everyone started laughing and gasping; some people clapped as the keeper released the indifferent eel back into the water. I stared at the eel in wonderment. I could barely breathe. "Daddy, Mom, did you see that!" I finally said after a few minutes.

"Yeah, baby, that was something else," my father said. His hand was still on my shoulder.

"How do you think he did that?" I said.

"Well, now Josie, I don't know," Daddy said. "Let's see

if we can figure that out." As if he had heard us, the man who had done the demonstration came out of an industrial-looking side door. My father took my hand, leaving Tick and Mom standing in front of the tank, and we walked up to him. My father said, "Excuse me, young man?"

"Yes, sir?" He turned around, ready to help.

"My daughter here is very interested in marine life and I wonder if you could tell her a little bit about how that electric eel functions. She's very smart and she wants to know."

I looked up at Daddy, my heart aching with embarrassment and love. The eel guy grinned and got down on one knee so he could talk directly to me. He launched into a long explanation of how it was mostly made up of organs that generated electricity and how those organs functioned. I absorbed some of it. But what I got most was the sense that my curiosity mattered—that guy on his knee in front of me and Daddy with his hand on my back, both trying to answer my questions. We probably talked for all of three minutes, but it was blissful. I walked back to Tick and Mom in a daze.

Tick was still staring raptly at the tank. After a few minutes, he spoke. "I want him to do it again," he said.

Daddy and Mom laughed. "Tick, you are something, boy. Soon as you do something you like once, damn if you don't want to do it again just a minute later," Daddy said.

"That's for sure," Mom agreed then smiled at me. "Did you get your question answered, miss?"

"Yeah, yeah I did. Thanks, Mom." She rested her hand on my head briefly and then we headed into the rest of the aquarium together, a family. The air was cool and smelled of salt water and closely packed humans.

We stayed at the aquarium for probably another two hours. We saw a lot of cool stuff but nothing as amazing as that eel. I did love the tropical fish—they didn't scare and thrill me like the eel had but I loved the way their colors asserted themselves. I used some of my allowance money to buy a poster in the gift shop of some Caribbean fish before we left. Tick bought a rubber eel and a little plastic goldfish that squirted water.

It was a warm early summer day, the air resting mildly on our skin, the way it sometimes seems to do before it gets too hot. When we got home, Mom told us to go play and went inside. Tick got a bucket, filled it with a hose, dragged it to the backyard, and threw his eel in. He spent some time lining up his army men around the edge of the bucket. He put two in as scuba divers. "Come on, Josie, play with me," he said. His eel dived and sloshed through the water as he made sizzling, fizzing sounds. Together we made up an elaborate story about an eel named Reggie who swam the seven seas and performed marvelous feats. No matter how assiduously Reggie was hunted, he always came battling back to defeat his many enemies. We played for a long time, getting soaking wet in the process. Finally, we took a break and sat side by side on the damp grass.

"That was something, huh, that eel?" I said. "I wish I could swim around with it."

"You'd get fried up!" Tick laughed.

"Maybe I could wear a special suit or something. You know, like on that old Jacques Cousteau show we saw. People go down there."

Tick pulled up a tuft of grass. "Yeah. I guess," he said.

"I wanna go down there."

"Yeah? I don't think they have eels like that in Lake Erie."

"No, dummy. I'd have to go where they live. But I wanna go down into the ocean. When I'm grown."

Tick didn't say anything. I could hear our parents' voices distantly from inside the house, but I couldn't tell what they were saying. The sun was warm on my back. We both sat silent, together, enjoying everything. Daddy didn't smell like beer. We had seen an electric eel. We'd all four had a good day. We sat there for a minute and tried to hold on to it. After a little while, Tick jumped up and said, "Come on. Reggie's back."

We stuck our hands back into the bucket and disappeared back into our own world. We didn't come in until Mom called us for dinner. Tick went to bed that night clutching his eel. And just before I fell asleep I said to my silent room, to wherever God was, quiet and fierce, "I am gonna go down there. I am."

Later, it hurt to remember that day. But I'd had it. We'd had it. It's worth something to have a day like that, a day that an angel comes to call.

Six

My father's fortieth birthday started the same way that many of our Saturdays did: with Tick and me sitting in the upstairs hall near our parents' door, playing together. One of our favorite games involved pretending to be eagles. It was a pretty simple game. We put our blankets on the floor and swirled them up into piles that looked kind of like nests and then we sat there, sometimes for a couple of hours, pretending to be majestic western birds. This mostly consisted of inventing and then telling each other about our various birdlike adventures and activities. Our interest in the stories we made up never waned. After Saturday-morning cartoons went into reruns, we'd even abandon the TV in order to play. I especially liked to play on the landing near my parents' room, so I could keep an eye on things—I was ever vigilant.

There had been no beer since before our trip to the aquarium a month before. Daddy came home on time every night and had dinner with the family and then read *Sounder* to Tick and me and told us how much it reminded him of his childhood—the grinding poverty and the one-room shack and the white people who were both curiously absent and whose rules dictated almost everything that ever happened. I remember looking at him after that like he was from another country. I couldn't imagine my big, stolid father a barefoot boy chasing after chickens. The night he finished reading it he said, "You see how those folks had nothing, right? That's why I want you both to get a scholarship to a private school. Only way I got out of that was through learning. You can go even farther. Nothing will hold you back if you keep learning." Then he hugged us both very hard. For that month, Tick and I fell asleep to our parents' soft voices conversing or the silence of them reading together—they didn't even watch much TV. Things were calm, but Tick still came into my bedroom every night and pushed Purrface out of the way and slept there himself, curled up like the cat he'd displaced.

• • •

THE MORNING OF MY father's birthday, Mom came out of the bedroom, tying her robe around her. We looked up from our game the minute she came out.

"What is all this?" she asked.

"We're eagles," said Tick, grinning. "These are our nests."

I held up a pink rubber ball that was swaddled in my nest. "This is my egg. It's gonna hatch any day now." I cawed—a quick, sharp scraggly sound—and Mom laughed. "What was that, Josie?"

"I'm the mother eagle protecting my egg. I gotta look out for it, right?"

"Right." She rubbed both of our heads. I loved when she was relaxed and affectionate like this. She smiled down at us. "Listen, it's your daddy's birthday so we have a lot to do. Can you two be my helpers today?" We both nodded. "Good," she said. "Well, little eagles, you need to clean up this mess. Breakfast will be ready pretty soon."

"Aw, Mom, five more minutes? It's Saturday. Come on." This came from Tick with his sweetest smile. I was already resigned to (and sometimes grateful for) Tick's ability to get around my mother. To get around most people really. There was just something about him—that angelic pout, his quick wit, his liveliness—that made you willing to do what he wanted. Sometimes his powers were used to the advantage of us both—that's when I was grateful. But when he was getting some privilege that I couldn't manage to wheedle? Oh, it made me furious.

"Okay, five more minutes. But then you need to come when I call."

"Okay, Mom."

We went back to our game. Daddy came out shortly afterward dressed for work; he was getting in some overtime, as he often did on Saturdays. "What the devil are you two doing?" He smiled. It wasn't the same as with Mom, perhaps because it was rarer and that made it more precious. We told him about the game and he said, "You know, the national bird was supposed to be the turkey, not the eagle." When he was in good spirits, he offered up odd little facts like this, the slight showing-off of a self-educated man.

"Yeah, Daddy?" Tick said, seizing the moment of connection. "That'd be pretty funny, eating the national bird for Thanksgiving." Daddy laughed and rubbed his head and went down to breakfast. We didn't say anything to each other, didn't acknowledge the good feeling. But it was on us like sunshine. Our mother didn't call us down for at least twenty minutes, too, so we got to play more.

When we came thundering down the stairs, Daddy and Mom were sitting at the table, silent. The air was a little still between them. We sat down and Mom gave us some slightly cold eggs and they continued to eat, not speaking to each other. Tick pressed his leg into mine, briefly. We ate fast. Then I thought that maybe Daddy was angry because we hadn't mentioned his birthday. "Happy birthday, Daddy!" I said and jumped up to hug him. "Yeah, Daddy, happy birthday," said Tick. My mother's back relaxed a bit and she said softly, "Happy birthday, Ray."

He smiled at us. "Y'all got something planned for me later?"

"We might. We might." This from Mom.

"Well, good. I'll be home early—round five or so." He stood up, pulled on his cap (one of those flat Kangol-style ones—very snappy), kissed each of us, and left. The air in the kitchen lightened suddenly. We were dismissed to go get dressed and come back down to help.

WE WORKED HARD THAT day. We baked a beautiful vanilla cake with white icing and helped Mom clean up the house and carefully wrapped the bottle of Old Spice we had bought him. (He never wore aftershave, but we loved to buy it for him. I used it for bath oil for my Barbies after he'd made his one-time-to-be-gracious use of it.) Mom cooked his favorite, smothered pork chops and string beans. She put on a beautiful pink dress—the color my father liked her best in—and put a little perfume behind her ears. And then we sat down in the living room to wait. He was supposed to be home in about half an hour. We sat. And sat. And sat. Five-thirty. Six. Six-thirty. Tick and I played old maid for a while but then we started to throw the cards at each other and yell for justice. Mom kept telling us to hush up. She sat by the window, looking out it as if she could will him home. The cake turned soggy under its warming frosting and the fat congealed on the gravy-covered pork chops and she looked out the window. At around seven-fifteen I couldn't stand it anymore. I said in a small voice, a smaller voice than I thought I possessed, "Mom, I'm hungry. Can we go ahead and eat?"

I couldn't read the look Mom gave me. My stomach rumbled and Tick and I looked at her, hardly able to breathe. Finally she sighed and said, "Yes, baby. Why don't we go on and eat. I don't know what could be keeping your father." So we sat and ate the cold pork chops and the greasy beans and I thought I might choke from everything we weren't saying and then it was seven-thirty and then it was eight and that's when he came in the door.

His eyes were red. He smelled like a brewery. He was weaving, just a tiny little bit. He was the only thing in the room that moved. He leaned on the doorframe. "Hey, y'all. Sarah, Josie, Tick. Listen. I had to work late and then Oscar and them wanted to go out for a drink and I *said* to them just one and . . ." Mom raised her hand.

"Josie and Tick, you better go on to your rooms." We got up and scooted up the stairs; Tick took my hand and held it very tightly. When we got to the landing where they couldn't see us, Tick refused to take another step.

"Come on, Tick, Mom said to go upstairs."

"We are upstairs."

"You know what I mean. All the way upstairs."

Tick's jaw set. "This is far enough. I ain't going up to my room. What if something happens?"

What if something happens. What would happen? How did he know the question that pressed under my skin every day, the question that never quite left? I stopped and led him by the hand to the edge of the landing so we could bear witness.

"Ray, what the hell am I supposed to think? You come in here on your own birthday three hours later than you said you would, drunk as hell. You stink." Mom was crying. "We worked so hard. The kids and I worked so hard to give you a nice birthday."

Daddy kept leaning on the doorframe. "Well, nobody *asked* you to do all this. I didn't have any birthday parties growing up. Didn't anybody care what year it was or how old I was."

"Well, now you do have people who care, Ray. We care so much. You should have seen those kids today. They worked so hard. They so want to make things nice for you. And you . . ." As she said the next words, she turned and swept the cake off the table and onto the floor. "You just treat it like so much trash."

Daddy stepped toward her and grabbed her wrist. "Go ahead," she said. "You want to be that low? Go ahead and hit me."

"I ought to," he said. "If a man can't go out and have a beer with his boys on his birthday without coming home to this shit. . . . I ought to hit you."

They stood there like that for what seemed like forever, though it was probably only a couple of minutes. But then he let go and sagged into the chair and said, not looking at her, "You better clean this mess up. I'm going back out. Tell the kids I said thanks."

"Thanks! Thanks!" She was screaming now. She had forgotten us. "You're just going to go back out and get drunker? What the hell is wrong with you?"

He stood up and put his hat back on. He had his hand on the doorknob. He said quietly, so quietly we almost couldn't hear, "I swear to God I don't know." And then he was gone.

Mom stood in the dining room breathing heavily for a few minutes after he left. Tick and I had come to sit on the top step. Tick put his head in my lap and started crying.

Then I started, too. That got her attention. She looked up and there we were.

"Oh, babies, I'm sorry," she said. "Listen, Daddy got hung up at work and he had to go back and get something he forgot. He's very sorry that he missed our party."

I stared at her. I couldn't believe that she would just lie like that. But maybe it was safer to believe that than to believe my own eyes. "What happened to the cake?" I said, my voice the still sound of winter.

"Oh, I was being silly. I picked it up and went to go move it and it just slipped out of my hands."

Tick was still crying. Mom squeezed in next to the two of us on the step. Tick turned his hot little head toward Mom and she cradled him, leaving my lap cold and damp. I let him go reluctantly. I never stopped looking at Mom. "So you dropped the cake," I said. Was she really going to stick with that story? That ridiculous story? We *saw* her. We *saw* them. But she looked back at me and said in a dead-even tone, "Yes, I did." I nodded once and squinched my eyes tight shut. Then I leaned to put my head on Tick's back. The truth was not to be spoken. I got that. The three of us sat there for a very long time.

Seven

Earlier that evening, my father sits on a barstool, pink neon lighting his dark skin. His buddy Oscar sits beside him. The arc of these evenings—and he has avoided having such an evening for a month or so—tends to be remarkably similar. They spend all day working the line, like so many black men did before them and like gradually decreasing numbers will after. The work is stupefying; their hands are stiff from performing the same actions over and over and over. Bend lift screw. Bend lift screw. Bend lift screw. The car doors slide past them in a never ending succession. Around four, he begins to think of that first beer, the cool shock to the tongue, the friendly fizz of it, and the lightness that follows in his chest. He thinks of the smooth sound of Motown burbling out of the jukebox, the warmth radiating from his friend's leg near his under the bar, the ease that exists in that dark room. Four-thirty comes and passes, the car doors keep sliding by, his hand keeps twisting screws in rhythmically. Until it is finally time to punch out.

It was his fortieth birthday. He had two children and a wife whom he loved very much. He had a job that ate a little bit of his spirit every day. He felt time passing, as do we all, and it scared him sometimes. He meant to go home that night. He really did. But it was his birthday. He had been doing so well, resisting that impulse for so long. What could one beer hurt?

He'd said to Oscar as they went into the bar, "I gotta get home, man. It's my birthday and they're expecting me home."

"It's your birthday, man? I didn't know that. All the more reason to buy you a beer today. Listen." Oscar turned to speak to the bartender. "This brother is—how old are you?"

"Forty."

"Forty today! I think this old man needs a boilermaker to celebrate!" Oscar clapped him on the back.

The sharp cold beer and the small warm glass of whiskey sat on the bar together, inviting him, all but smiling at him. Marvin Gaye eased out of the jukebox; Oscar grinning beside him. He'd go after this one. He'd just have this one drink this time. This time he was sure he'd be able to do it.

THREE HOURS LATER. "OH, shit, man. I gotta go." The same heaviness in his words that there always was after the one, two, three, how many beers? He made his way to the door, weaving slightly, the careful walk of a man who had done this many times. He drove home very slowly, peering hard at each stoplight and hesitating before he hit the gas. When he walked into the house, the children, the wife, the cake, the screaming, the dashed expectations. The weight of it was all too much. He said cruel things, none of which he meant. *How can I treat them like this?* he thought. *They just wanted to give me a nice birthday.* But the vicious words were out before they could be called back and made into anything else. He had to leave after that—his shame was too great. He felt all of our eyes, big and dark and frightened, boring through his back as he left.

He didn't have a place in mind to go when he walked out the door. He guessed that Oscar had left the bar by this time; the magic was gone anyway. His buzz was being replaced by a familiar, grinding wretchedness.

He got in the car and drove, slowly, to an open mini-grocery. He paid for a six-pack. Then he drove down to the parking lot near Lake Erie. He didn't know exactly why he chose the lake, except he knew that the parking lot would be deserted. He was able to pull up close enough to see the water from his car window. He opened the window to let in the warm spring air. He could hear the slap, slap, slap of the small lake waves. But he was afraid to get out of the car. He sat in the front seat and opened can after can of beer until they were all gone. He was too drunk and miserable even to climb into the backseat and lie down. He finally fell asleep in the front seat—passed out really—until the dawn's light pierced his eyes. When he got home, his beautiful wife said, "I called you in sick already." She didn't say another word to him for the rest of the day. He spent much of the day lying in bed, staring at the ceiling, vowing never to drink again, a vow he did not keep. His hands were clenched to fists. His eyes were dry.

Eight

After that night, the brakes were off. My father was rarely without a beer in his hand. My mother retreated to a sad silence that Tick and I could rarely get her to break. Time went on and time went on. We became teenagers. We both got scholarships to Dean, that prep school I mentioned. We didn't tell anyone there about what home was like. We just went on. We never talked about what was happening at home and whatever my parents were thinking; they certainly didn't share with us. So to tell about this last part, I'm going to have to make a bigger imaginative leap than I have thus far—bigger, perhaps, than even seems plausible. But this world is full of implausible things. So I'm going to let them speak through me. My mother first.

I NEVER COULD GET Tick and Josie to see that a marriage doesn't come apart all at once. That deciding whether or not to stay or go is the most complicated thing in the world. Especially if sometimes you can still see glimpses of the person you married. That person keeps darting out of reach, washed away or shut away, but you keep hoping he might come back. You keep thinking that if you just hang in there, you might get him back.

Aside from how lonely it got to be with Ray, I was bored. I missed nursing. I missed being useful, doing for people other than my family. And once the kids got big and got themselves those scholarships and started running with a whole different crowd out at that school, well, I just felt like I didn't have a place anymore. It was hard, watching Josie at that school, watching her fight to be the girl she wanted to be: a girl who loved something that really seemed to be only for white men. Watching her, I started to think that I wanted to set an example of a woman who did what she needed to do, what she wanted to do, without worrying too much about what other people thought.

But the main thing was that the man I married was so long gone, and I just didn't want to pretend he wasn't anymore. He sat in front of that television like a statue, the beer just flowing through him. I'd have asked him to leave the bedroom, but the house wasn't big enough. There was nowhere else for him to sleep. So we slept as far away from each other as we possibly could, hanging on to the edges of our queen-size mattress. I was a little afraid of being alone. But really, I was alone already in all the important ways. Why not make it official?

So when Josie was a senior, I did a couple of things. I found out what I'd need to do to get back into nursing. I'd been away so long that my license had lapsed; I had to take some classes and an exam to renew it before I could even begin to look for work. But I also saw that the jobs were out there. So quietly, without saying anything to Ray, I started applying to classes for the fall. I hid the forms in my underwear drawer and filled them out, bit by bit, while he was at work.

I didn't keep everything from him, though. I did tell him that I had started volunteering at the Boys & Girls Club that summer a couple of times a week. He was at work and the house was as kept as it was going to get and Josie was gone to Florida for the summer—she'd gotten herself into a high school oceanography/marine biology program. Judging from her occasional letters, she was as happy as could be. Tick? Well, God only knew what Tick was doing. He came home occasionally to get food and wash his clothes, but that was about it. He barely spoke to me, and he didn't say a mumblin' word to Ray. It was like we were his not all that comfortable boarding house. The family of one of his new white friends with money had a membership to a golf club and Tick got a job working in the concession stand there. At first, it seemed that getting a job would be good for him—get him out of the house, teach him some responsibility. But I didn't realize that he'd use it as a way to get free of us. He would come home from work, eat something, some of the time, standing in front of the refrigerator, foot tapping, and then he'd be gone again. Never a proper meal. Never a proper conversation. A stranger.

So that's what made me decide to start volunteering at the Boys & Girls Club. The days were so full of hours and so empty of affection or pleasure. I had a few friends but no one that I felt I could tell the truth of my life to. So after a while, the cups of coffee turned stale and bitter in my mouth. How many times can you shine a table that already shines, sweep a floor that's free of dust? No. I had to do something else. No one ever touched me anymore. No one seemed happy to see me anymore. No one wanted me anymore.

I loved watching the kids pelting around outside or helping them inside as they wriggled, working on craft projects, glue and Popsicle sticks everywhere. They reminded me of Tick and Josie, years ago, even though these kids tried to be tough: Some of them used rough language and swaggered a little bit. But mostly they were young and sweet and the street hadn't gotten to them yet. Even the ones who tried to act so hard weren't—not really. They weren't rude or disrespectful. Some of them would be later. But they weren't yet. They hadn't learned what the world was going to think of them, a bunch of black kids without a lot of money.

One of my favorites was a little girl named Ayesha. She had two puffy braids (just the way I used to do Josie's hair) with those rubber-band holders that end with plastic balls. She had a serious, thoughtful air, and she carried a notebook shoved under her arm. Her glasses were always sliding down her nose. She wore the same faded red sweatshirt every day. And she sat in the corner of the playground, writing and writing. I watched her for days. Finally, I got up the nerve to go over and talk to her. "What are you working on so hard?" I asked.

"My notebook," she said, her eyes clear and sure.

"My daughter used to like to keep a notebook that had a list of all the plants and fish and things that she found outside and at the beach. What do you put in your notebook?" I found myself sliding down to sit next to her, even though it had been many years since I'd sat on the ground like that myself. I remembered getting up with dusty knees and never worrying about what people would say. It was a long time ago that I was that free. Ayesha looked at me as though she was considering whether or not I was to be trusted. She decided I was. "I write down stuff I see. Stuff I think about. I got the idea from this book *Harriet the Spy*."

"I don't know that book. What's it about?"

Ayesha looked uncertain if she should tell. Then she kept talking, getting more and more excited. "Well, it's about this girl Harriet. She's a white girl who lives in New York City. And she wears a red sweatshirt—that's why I got one—and she writes down everything she sees. But then her friends find out that she wrote some mean stuff about them and they get really angry. The things she says are true, but they're kind of mean." She paused for breath. "But then Mrs. Henderson, here's the crazy part. She has this grown-up friend, this lady who stays with her, and she tells Harriet that she has to *lie*. That sometimes you have to lie about things. Do you think that's true?" She looked up at me, her eyes intent and thoughtful. She was clutching her notebook to her chest.

I looked out at the kids playing on the playground and I listened to their whoops and shouts. I felt that it was important that I be honest with this child. It had been a while since I'd been honest with a child. "Well, I think that's right. Sometimes you do have to lie. Sometimes the truth hurts and it causes pain for no good reason. Sometimes. Then I think it's right to lie. But you have to be careful.

It's a trap, lying like that too much." My heart sped up as I talked, even though we weren't moving at all. Why was my heart racing like that? I could feel the girl's warm body next to mine. "Sometimes you do a body more harm than good trying to protect them. Sometimes the lies get to be too much. You know?"

"So you think it's okay to lie sometimes?"

"Yes, I do. Sometimes. As you get older, it gets easier to sort out when those times might be."

Ayesha nodded gravely. "My mama says don't lie. Period. But I don't know. When I read that in *Harriet,* I thought that might be true. I could think of times when that would be true." She stood up, suddenly. "Can I go play now?"

"Sure. Sure, Ayesha. You go on now. You can leave your notebook here."

"Don't look in it. It's private. That's the other thing I learned from the book: Keep your notebook private."

"I won't look, I promise." She ran off, her braids bobbing, her feet almost kicking her own behind as she ran. I placed my hand on her notebook but I didn't open it. I thought about what I had said about lying, if that's what I truly believed. How did you know when enough was enough, when taking care of someone or something through a lie wasn't the right thing to do anymore? How could a child tell the difference? How could I? I felt the oddest thrumming start in the soles of my feet as I watched Ayesha play. I didn't know what it was. I just felt it.

The rest of the day I kept thinking about Ayesha's face while we were talking, the way she looked as if she were trying to figure out the weight of the world. Some kids begin to see that there *is* a weight of the world before others do—Josie was like that. I always felt for her a little. But I always admired it, too. It helped her be clear about things. She saw how things were at home and she got the hell out—as much as a high school girl could anyway. There was a kind of clarity in that.

The Boys & Girls Club wasn't far from our house so I always walked there and back. It was an unseasonably warm day and everything was iridescent. The sycamores on our street arched gracefully over the quiet sidewalks. I waved at the neighbors, Henrietta Boyd with that yappy dog of hers and old Mr. Emerson, who used to get after the kids so when they ran across his lawn. They waved and helloed back, their familiar voices floating by. I could feel each footfall on the pavement. Everything was starkly outlined in front of me as if it were under glass. When I arrived home, I put my key in the lock, opened the door, and entered the house. It was cool and dark inside. I went into the kitchen and Ray was sitting there, home from work early, a cigarette burning in front of him, a beer sweating onto the table. I wasn't surprised to see him. He was staring out the window. I had loved him so much once. I still would, if he'd let me. But I had that feeling in the soles of my feet and I suddenly knew what it was telling me. I was through lying for him. I was through lying to him. I ought never to have started. This wasn't one of those things it was right to lie about. It never had been. But I was going to stop right now.

"Ray?" I said, my voice so firm that it surprised me. "Ray. Something has to change, Ray. You need to leave." He turned to look at me. The thrumming in my soles stopped. I was hard, still, ready for whatever lay ahead.

Nine

When Sarah asked me to leave, I wasn't all that surprised. That blade had been coming toward my neck for a while. Can't say I didn't deserve it. It was almost a relief.

When she told me, I was sitting at the kitchen table, just sitting with a beer. When I thought about it—I couldn't stand to think about it much—I knew that I was spending a lot more time that way than I ever had before. I got up and went to work and I always did my job and I went to that factory and lifted those doors and supported my family and held my head up. But it used to be that I did other things after work. I read all the time. And I had a wood shop downstairs. I made the chairs in the kids' bedrooms—my father taught me when I was just a kid myself. I'd always liked making something from the ground up, especially after a few years on the line, when all I did was make part of something, part of something, part of something. When the kids were little, I played with them sometimes. And of course, I used to try to write. It was hard. But I used to try.

But by the time she asked me to leave, the main thing I did with my time was watch TV, letting it wash over me. It was getting hard for me to concentrate on a book. I was always wondering how long it would be before I felt like it was okay to get up and get another beer. Sometimes I could stay focused enough to reread something light. Nothing difficult like Spenser or Milton or Ellison. But things that went down easy and that I found soothing, stuff like James M. Cain and Dashiell Hammett. I read *The Postman Always Rings Twice* and *The Maltese Falcon* over and over. For a while, I told myself that it was because I was tired from work or the kids were driving me crazy or this or that or the other. But the truth was, I couldn't concentrate. I was letting the books go, as much as I loved them.

Here's what Sarah said to me, her eyes shining so positive and clear that it made her beautiful to look at. I never told her that I felt that way still. But it made me happy to look at her, even as she said: "Ray, you need to leave."

I looked up from where I'd been staring at the table.

"What do you mean, I need to leave?" I slid my hand across the table, feeling the aged smoothness of the wood. It calmed me, somehow.

"I mean that you have sat around here with that damn beer for all of our children's childhoods. I mean that no one has touched me in ten years except the kids. I mean that you've gained thirty pounds and you smell like a brewery and I don't even want you near me." Now she started crying, standing there in her immaculate kitchen, in the home we made together, where we used to love each other. Where I loved her still. But I wasn't doing right. I never did right anymore. She didn't try to wipe away her tears. "I mean that I miss you but it seems like there's no getting you back, so you might as well go on and leave altogether. I've still got some kind of life to lead. I've got to lead it without you. I don't want to. But I have to."

Even though I knew she was right, I hadn't reached bottom yet. Not yet. So this is what I said—I'll never forget it. It took a long time to forgive myself. I took a swig of the beer and said, "What do you mean, you have to? Haven't I been here, right here, putting up with these kids and putting up with the way you run the house and never doing what I want to do?" I started shouting. "What *I* want to do for all these years. I could have done something, if it wasn't for . . ." I trailed off. What was I gonna say? What were those great things I could have done? How did they—this woman that I loved and these kids we made together—stop me? They hadn't stopped me. Suddenly, I felt exhausted. "I'm sorry, Sarah." I stood up and took a step toward her and she backed away like I might hit her. Something I'd never done in my life. But then, she didn't know me anymore. I didn't even know myself. "I want you out of here by tomorrow," she said, her voice deadly level. "I'll tell Tick and Josie."

I didn't have another word to say. I just turned away from her and walked up the stairs.

Part Two

Ten

My name is Edmund but everybody calls me Tick. I'm an alcoholic. I've been in and out of these meetings too many times to count. I know these damn steps by heart. I just can't live 'em. Well, I don't have the willingness yet. Don't know when I'm gonna get it. I'm sitting here, sharing, because I'm trying again. It's been three months since I've had a drink. I've been drinking since I was about fifteen. Problem is, I like drinking. It's cost me almost every damn thing I have—but I still love that first taste. It's what comes after it that's bitter.

I was married for a while. My ex-wife's name is Theresa. She has long light-brown dreadlocks and the sweetest smile I've ever seen. I know it's hard to believe, looking at me now, that I was once something. That I once had something.

People who loved me and looked out for me. A job that I liked. A wife whose good heart I miss so much. Even though I won't ever see her again.

We met at a bar, of course. Ironic, right? I was on my third beer, feeling loose and good. She was with her girlfriends, nursing a seltzer. She didn't drink much, I found out later. She wasn't preachy about it. She'd drink wine or a gin and tonic once in a while—she didn't *mind* drinking. But when she started to get drunk, she would stop. She had the brakes everybody in this room doesn't have.

We got to talking. She worked at the Cleveland Museum in the Africana Department as a curatorial assistant. I had just started with the Cavs, at the lowest rung on the ladder of the trainers. But I loved being at all the games, hanging out with the guys (even though, a lot of the time, I was just fetching ice and watching the more senior trainers work). I loved how we'd all go out after a game for a beer or two or four. I loved how the night would come on and then pass. It was 2000 and things were looking pretty rough for the Cavs. LeBron? Well, he was still a high-school kid—one hell of a high-school kid but not ready to go pro yet. So wasn't much happening with the Cavs. Even so, being around the players, around guys who play at that pro level—well, there's nothing like it. You can't imagine it. I was twenty-five. Everything was in front of me. Sometimes somebody would have a little bit of cocaine with them and they'd do it in the bathroom of whatever bar we were in. I didn't do it every time, but I liked it. I liked the way it cut through the warm fuzziness of alcohol, gave everything a hyped-up brilliant sheen. Made me feel like the king of everything. It was a great combination. It was a great time. I was young and good-looking and about to be accomplished. That's when I met Theresa.

It all went very smoothly for a long time. There was the dating, there was the love, there was the living together, there was the wedding, there was us, and through it all, I was drinking, but it was just part of the job. Just part of the job, I told her. I told myself that, too. I told myself that as we started to fight more and more. I told myself that as she began to turn away from me when I tried to kiss her and then I stopped trying to kiss her. I told myself that when one night coming home late and fuzzy-headed from beer and cocaine turned into two, and then three and then four and then I lost count of how many nights, oh hell, it was every night, every night I was away from her, every night I was drinking. I told myself that as I shouted at her, a man I didn't even recognize myself to be, shouting like a madman at my sweet brown wife with her sweet brown dreads and her delicate hands. I told myself that as she cried. I told myself that as she packed her bags, as she laid her hand on my cheek and said, "Baby, I can't live like this anymore, and you won't get any help. So I've got to go." I stood at the door for a while after she left, looking at the space in the parking lot of our apartment building where her car had been. And then I went back to our apartment and opened the refrigerator and got a beer, sharp and cold and kind, and one by one by one, I drank myself into my second stint in rehab. And that's why I'm here. I don't want to pick it up again. I want to get out of my mother's basement. I want to stay sober. I wish I didn't have to take things one day at a time. I want to know right now that I'm gonna stay away from that bottle for good. I wish to God there was some way to know for sure.

Eleven

Tick was so grateful to the Cavs for taking him back. He hadn't been at all sure that they would. Before he went to rehab, he'd been missing staff meetings, telling players to ice body parts that they should have been heating and vice versa. He was working with a hangover so often that he was terrified he'd hurt someone—cause some kind of harm to those million-dollar legs and arms. When he got nervous, he drank. And that just made it harder the next day and on and on.

He couldn't believe it when he was first hired onto the training staff of the Cavs. He loved basketball and he was good at it. He loved playing, the running and sweating and passing and jumping—everything about it. But well before high school was over, it became apparent that he was only good for a kid at a midwestern prep school. Which wasn't good enough for the big time. So he applied to Penn State and got in. He went there. Mostly because of the football and basketball—he thought he'd at least like watching, maybe play intramural. He did for a while, too. He majored in physical education. And partying. He did enough of that to have declared a double major. When he thought about it, which he didn't much, he felt a kind of wonder that he'd made it out of college at all with so many lost nights. But he charmed and cajoled and last-minute studied his way to a degree, and then he figured out what he wanted to do with his dented basketball dream. He wanted to work with athletes—pro if possible, he'd take what he could get if not. He wanted to be close to those bodies and understand the power that they had that he didn't. And somehow, he knew that he'd never make it through applying and getting into and finishing a master's program in physical therapy if he didn't sober up. So he went to rehab for the first time and dried out and went to meetings. For a few years, he sobered up and found out that he was good at finding where it hurt in a body and helping to ease the ache. When he found his way to the position with the Cavs, it was like God was calling his name. It was a chance to be near the players, a chance not to be behind a desk. He knew, from the moment he sat next to one of the players after a game and massaged a cramp out of a calf, that he had come home.

He hadn't been around this many guys who could have been his brothers since he'd left for high school. Yeah, they were all much, much younger than he was, with their Escalades and their boomin' systems and their easy, disposable way with women. (One time he heard one of the guys say to another, "Yeah, girls are just like Kleenex. It's always another one in the box.") But he liked it—the towel snaps and the rough language. It was so tonally different from his high school. He found himself slipping back into speech patterns that he'd left in the old neighborhood once he'd spent enough time at Dean. Adding some new wrinkles, too. Seemed like there was some new slang, some new name for something or other every day.

Saying that he worked for the Cavs came in pretty handy in bars, too. There'd been no steady girl since his divorce—he just couldn't settle down. And the women who hung around the team? Well, let's just say they weren't the settling-down type. (An aside: I adored Theresa—she was a fantastic sister-in-law.) At first, even though he wasn't one of the players, he was still together enough and good-looking enough to pull the prettier, more appealing women. But as the booze got out in front of him (again, so sneakily, so slowly, but again), he started to find that women he was fucking in joyless trysts that he often could not recall in the morning were just depressing. Crass and dumb and overly made-up and prone to belching and farting and then laughing about it. They had rough skin and smelled of gin or the edgy tang of cocaine. There was nothing to talk with them about—most of the time, they were both too drunk to talk anyway. For the most part, he didn't even find them pretty. But he fucked them anyway. That was the really sad thing. He felt such contempt for them and for himself as he slid in between their waiting open legs. But he couldn't stop.

His first day back at the job, he was awake shortly before the alarm went off. He lay there for a while, feeling the ceiling press down toward his head, but then it was time to get up and get going. He rolled over to his nightstand and picked up the Alcoholics Anonymous big book that he kept there. He loved the old-fashioned, kind of corny way it was written: "Half measures availed us nothing. We stood at the turning point. We asked His protection and care with complete abandon." He offered a brief prayer to whatever was out there that he could do this. He sighed, put the book down, and made his bed. In his time at the rehab, he had become a master bed-maker; hospital corners and sheets so tight that you could, in fact, bounce a quarter off them. He tried once and was oddly pleased to find that it was possible. At Riverrun, they made a very big deal of the addict or alcoholic's need to start taking care of him- or herself, to start living by the rules, to start having order in their lives. He stood admiring his tightly made bed and tried not to think about the fact that he was thirty-four years old and living in his mother's basement. He looked at himself in the mirror while he was shaving and said, "One day at a time," out loud. It was not as reassuring as he hoped it would be. This day would include using his mother's computer to look at apartment ads so he could begin to see how hard it was going to be to save up enough to get one. How many thousands of dollars would it take to be a man again? He rinsed the lather from his face.

He went upstairs. His mother had set out breakfast for him, just like she used to do for Daddy. Scrambled eggs and bacon and slightly dark toast. He was hungry, which was a check mark on the good side. So often, for so long, he woke up sickened by the thought of food. It got so bad that he started to find it peculiar that some people actually wanted and enjoyed breakfast. That was one of the first things he had to learn at rehab: to eat normal food at normal times. To think of something besides his next drink, his next hit. At rehab, they were treated much like children, all the rules to follow and good behavior to learn. Now that he was home, it wasn't much different. As he sat at Mom's table, he felt about six years old. She touched the back of his neck as he hunched over his coffee. Her hand was warm and dry. His eyes stung at her touch.

"Did you sleep all right, Tick?"

"Yeah, Mom. Good. Thanks."

She sat down across from him, her hands folded around her own cup of coffee. She looked at him without saying anything for a few long minutes. Then she sighed and said, "You sure you're all right now?"

How could he tell her the truth? That you didn't know. He didn't know. "I'm okay right now, Mom. I'm going to a meeting tonight if I don't get hit by a bus on the way to work. That's all I can tell you. You know what they say."

She looked genuinely curious. "What? What do they say?"

"One day at a time. That's the only way I can take it now."

"Oh." She looked disappointed, as though she'd expected him to offer her some deeper revelation. "Your father says that to me all the time when we talk. I don't know how you all do it."

"Only way to do it, Mom. Only way I can see, anyway."

"Mmm." She sipped her coffee and looked distantly out the window. Silence fell over the kitchen. He put his mug down and stood up to leave. He could hear a sparrow singing outside. His mother seemed to be lit from within, but he supposed it was just the sunlight through the window, hitting her at the right angle. He leaned down to kiss her goodbye. "I'm sorry, Mom. I'm sorry about everything." She nodded and pressed her hand to his back, briefly. Then he left.

Somehow, he had hung on to his car. His mother had kept it in her driveway, and he was able to make payments on it from Riverrun for the time he was there. It nearly cleaned him out, but he needed to keep some vestige of independence, something that would allow him to get around the city, to be a man alone. He thought of nothing as he drove to work. He eased up to every yellow light with the caution of an old man wearing a hat (his friend Josh had once told him that old men in hats were the slowest, most cautious drivers; anecdotal evidence proved that to be true). He pulled into the basement parking lot of the arena feeling a little breathless, as though he'd just run an obstacle course. It had been some time since he'd been behind the wheel sober.

He had to meet with the head trainer who was his boss first, of course. Of the many people he'd let down, sometimes Tick felt worst about having let down Bob Trumbull. He was large and dark brown and serious of manner. He never raised his voice and he always got what he wanted. Except from Tick. He'd wanted him to succeed—Tick could feel it in the fatherly looks he gave him, the deeply concerned way he'd ask about how things were going. He'd been left hanging in the wind by the way Tick ended up coming into work so hungover and shaky that the player he was to work with refused to let Tick touch him. "Fuck if I'm letting that fool fuck up my leg" was the graceless but not inaccurate way that he put it. Bob saw Tick's crash coming for a while but it still hurt when he had to bring the whip down.

So now they sat uncomfortably across from each other at Trumbull's desk. Trumbull kept bending and unbending a paper clip. Tick sat on his hands. "So," said Trumbull. "Welcome back."

"Thanks." Tick felt as though he ought to say something more but he couldn't think what that might be.

"You feel ready to be back? Like you'll be able to stay focused?"

"I'm going to do my best, Bob. I think I'm ready. I did a lot of thinking while I was away. I want to do things different now. I want to do them right."

Bob bent his paper clip again, wordlessly. "Well, we're glad to have you back, Tick. But I can't let you near the players again until I have a chance—until *we* have a chance—to see that you're really back and ready. These young men are very valuable commodities and they've got to be handled carefully—kind of like racehorses." A slight smile crossed his face at this, and then he was serious again. "They have to feel totally comfortable with whoever's working with them. They have to have absolute trust. So we'll need you to do support work for a while—cleaning up the whirlpool, working with supplies, things like that." He didn't look at Tick as he said this.

Tick nodded. His heart rested heavily somewhere just below his belly button. No player contact. Cleaning out the whirlpool, a nasty job that no real trainer would do. And he was gonna be doing it. He wanted to lay his head down on the cool wooden surface of Trumbull's desk and close his eyes. He wanted to hit something. He knew it wouldn't solve anything, but he wanted a drink. But rather than do any of those things, he only nodded. One day at a time. Right. One minute at a time. Right.

Twelve

My name is Ray and I'm an alcoholic. It took me a long time to be able to sit in a room like this and say those words. I had to lose almost everything I loved before I could say that. I had to cause so much damage before I could say it.

Sometimes hitting bottom isn't a dramatic thing. There isn't a car accident. There isn't a death. There is just the moment when you sit there with the bottle and you say to yourself, "I can't do this anymore." I had that moment in the dirty, depressing apartment I moved into after Sarah, my wife, asked me to leave. I couldn't sleep—I'd had a few—and I found this old picture of me and Sarah. It must have been taken not long after we met. I had a book under one arm and the other arm around her. We were smiling at each other like two people who had spent the night spooned together and woke up happy to be together, eager for what the new day would bring. How could I have thrown her away? I rolled over, got out of bed, and dug out the phone book. I called and got the address and time of the nearest AA meeting. It wasn't until the next morning. I sat awake the rest of the night, getting drunk, watching television, catching broken moments of sleep while sitting up. And then I went to that meeting, still smelling of beer. I didn't know what would happen next. But at least I walked through the door.

Once you get willing, then things can begin to open up. That's how it's been for me anyway. I slipped once, a few years ago—started thinking I had it all under control. But after that, I surrendered again and good things started to come. I've got a life now, volunteer down at the library, got friends in these rooms, got stuff going on. But not everything's right. Some wounds take longer to heal.

I've got a daughter. Her name is Josie. She's grown now, a marine biologist; studies fish, studies the ocean. I'm so proud of her. When she was a little girl, she was always fascinated by the water. I used to watch her out in the backyard. She doesn't know that I ever looked at her that closely. But I did, sometimes. She could turn on the hose and watch that water run out of it for hours on end. Or when I had to water the lawn, she always wanted to help me: to hold the hose or be a part of it somehow. Her brown legs all covered with sparkling drops of water, such a beautiful child.

One time, when Josie was eleven or so, she talked me into going down to the beach with her. I was pretty deep into the drinking by then, too; it was definitely an everyday thing. But I could still be persuaded by her smile.

I was a little high, just feeling good, not over the edge or anything. It was a sunny day, and she had been riding her bike around the block the way she did. She loved to do that. I was sitting on the porch, watching the day go by, and her mama and her brother, Tick, were off somewhere, and she pulled her bike up in front of me and said, "Daddy, you wanna go down to the lake with me? You never go. Wanna go with me today?"

And I said yes. I got into the car and settled a beer in a paper bag between my knees. I thought it would be nice to look at the water and hold it and watch her and sip. She looked at the bag once, but she didn't say anything. Just hopped into the front seat next to me. She was getting leggy, looking more and more like her mama every day. She wore her hair in two braids, and one was coming undone. She had a serious look on her face. "So, little miss," I said, "what is it you do at the lake so much?"

She turned from the window to look at me and her face

brightened. "I like to skip rocks. And I like to look at stuff I find. It's not like the ocean. I really want to see the ocean sometime. There's way more stuff living in the ocean. But sometimes I can see a good fish or some vegetation or something." Vegetation. How about that? Eleven years old and talking like that, so smart. But the kind of smart she was seemed to have no end. I had my limits and I wasn't all that interested in the physical world, in understanding it and finding out where each piece of it fit together. She was. She wanted to know every bit of it. Started keeping lists of things around her—leaves, rocks, the different animals she saw—not that we had many, living right in the center of the city. But whatever she saw, she wrote down as soon as she could write. And you couldn't keep her away from those nature shows on TV. Anything she could watch she would, especially stuff about the ocean. She spoke again, interrupting my thoughts: "I like the water on my feet, too. The way it feels. I love the way it feels to be underwater." She fell silent. "How come you don't like the beach, Daddy?"

"Didn't grow up around it. Don't like being wet." I took a little taste. Growing up like I did, down south in one of those blink-and-you'd-miss-it little towns, I never did learn to swim anyway. She didn't know that, and I was embarrassed to tell her. Sarah had made sure that the kids knew how to swim. We both thought they needed to learn everything they could; that they should go to good schools and learn everything that would help them feel comfortable wherever they went. I'd spent so much of my life feeling uncomfortable. I didn't want that for my children. "I'm glad to be going there with you though, little bit. Real glad."

She smiled a small smile. We pulled into the parking lot and got out.

There were just a few cats out fishing, casting their lines over and over again into the greenish water. The air was very clear—"Fresh as if issued to children on a beach." That's what Virginia Woolf wrote in *Mrs. Dalloway.* I like her stuff, especially *To the Lighthouse.* I like a lot of writers that people don't think a guy like me would like. We got out of the car and Josie ran down to the rocks along the shore, yelling, "Come on, Daddy, come on!" I followed slowly, still sipping, still feeling pretty good. It was, I dunno, my sixth beer? My seventh?

She was taking her shoes off and wading into the water. She wasn't afraid at all. I stood on the shore, a safe distance from all that water, just watching her. The sound of the waves was kind of nice, I had to admit. I found a rock to sit on—didn't want to get sand in my pockets. And I didn't go so far as to take off my shoes. Josie ran and splashed and picked stuff up and put it down, perfectly content. I don't know how long this went on. Peaceful.

After a while, she came up to me and grabbed me by the hand. "Come on in, Daddy. Just take your shoes off. It's really great, you'll see." And she squatted down, like the little girl she was, and exuberantly started untying my shoes.

I nearly kicked her in the face. That's how fast I got up. She fell over backward onto her rump and looked up at me, already starting to cry. "No, damn it. I hate the water. I'm not going in there. If I want to take my shoes off, I'll do it myself. Damn it. Damn it. I don't want to go in the water, okay?"

Her face, her beautiful face just crumpled. I would have given anything to explain. I would have given anything to have that moment back and be gentle with her. I would have given anything not to have done what I'd just done. But I was drunk and I couldn't stop. I couldn't think. I ain't gonna blame it on the booze, because that's the kind of cop-out I've learned not to take in these rooms. No, I hurt my child myself. Me and my drunk ass. I was so scared. I couldn't let her see that. So I let her cry in the sand for a little while instead. After a while I said, "We better get on back, Josie. Your mama's gonna wonder where we are. Stop, girl. You aren't hurt." And that's all I said. That's all I ever said. That's the way I left it. If only I could have explained. I think that's when I started to lose her. Right at that moment.

I've got a son, too. Name of Edmund, but we call him Tick. He takes after me. Smart as you please—and a stone drunk. I don't know when it started. I was too drunk myself to see at the time. I couldn't help him. I couldn't even help myself. And I hadn't let go. He's drunk away almost everything now, and he uses other stuff besides. It breaks my heart. He's sober for now and I pray for him, but I don't know. I don't know if he's got what it takes to stay clean. It's a long road and he's got to walk it. No one can walk it for him—I learned that in these rooms. Even so . . . Lord, how I wish I could do it for him. With all my heart I wish it.

Thirteen

As long as I can remember, I've liked being out of the house. Whatever house it was. When I was a kid, I rode a school bus about fifteen miles away from home to the Dean school. I usually sat in the back and tried not to hear the cool kids talking about me—my hair or my clothes or something, everything that was wrong with me. The school bus didn't even come to our neighborhood—Mom had to drive me up into Cleveland Heights and then I'd wait there for the bus and then it was another hour (with all the stops) before we got there. And I always stayed after for science club or catching up on homework or even, for a little while, field hockey (those skirts!). In the summers, I went to camp (I got scholarships and did work study and stuff), and then when I got older, to whatever academic or aquatic summer program would have me. I worked to earn spending money, too—babysitting, restaurant hostessing, waitressing at local diners. Anything to be out of the house. Home and all it requires—the bills, the organizing, the talking to your loved ones—that stuff makes me nervous.

As you might imagine, this skittishness has made married life kind of tough. But then I never expected to be a wife. By the time I met Daniel, when I was thirty-three, I was pretty sure I wasn't going to get married. I had come to think that perhaps I was just too odd. Too black in a white profession. Too female in a male profession. Too in love with my work to love another person. Did I really want to spend my whole life with someone else? Genetically, we are only 1.23 percent different from chimpanzees. And they are not at all monogamous. Why should we be any different? That's what I believe. You'd think that I'd have raised this topic with my husband, my discomfort with monogamy. But somehow I've always been shy about doing that, as fundamental as it is. Scared, I guess. I'm scared a lot of the time.

There is a small part of me that suspects I got married because I was tired of looking around, tired of the dry spells of being single, tired of the game. Daniel appeared right at that time. He loved me. And I loved him. But he loved me more.

Although I was ready to stop running around when I met Daniel, there is one thing I miss: sexual variety. I love sex and I'm enthusiastic about it and so I didn't have much trouble finding people to have it with, even though what they say about most scientists' social skills is true. Talking to other people—generally a good preamble to getting into bed with them—is often not something they are particularly good at. But I can do what I need to do to make certain things happen. If I have to talk, I'll talk. If I have to flirt, I'll flirt. I'll even enjoy it. Ever since I had my first lover when I was sixteen and even before that when I started to figure this whole thing out, I knew that sex was going to be a way to an essential mystery, something it would take me a long time to understand and even longer to get tired of. This is going to sound silly, but I have Prince to thank for this. Me and my friend Deena snuck into a screening of *Purple Rain* one weekend when we were hanging around the Randall Park Mall and, frankly, I was never the same after that. Until then, my crushes had mostly been chaste fantasies of adventure with one passing teen idol or another—we were spies together, we climbed mountains together, sometimes the boy of the week would take my hand. But after I watched Prince weep and moan and smile his way through "Purple Rain" (And don't even get me started on "The Beautiful Ones." Amazing.) something crossed over in me. I hadn't thought about kissing a boy much, until that moment. Even when I lay on my bed thinking about Theo from *The Cosby Show* for hours and hours, I thought of *being* in his presence, not of kissing or anything further. But after that movie, it all made sense. Touching another person's body would be the point of it all. It wasn't like I didn't know about sex. My mother was unusually frank about that kind of thing—maybe because of having been a nurse. She gave me the whole rundown when I turned twelve. I found the mechanics of it very weird. But now I got it. Why wouldn't you want to do all that? All that kissing and stuff? Why wouldn't you want to be as close as you could to another person's glow, when you felt it? I still think that, to tell the truth. It makes being married hard.

My lovers weren't scientists, mostly. Sometimes this made for limited dinner table chat. But sometimes I wasn't very interested in a lot of talk anyway. Often I just wanted skin to skin, the smell of it, the textures and the sounds and the animal pleasure, the feel of the sheets under my back, my head on someone's chest, the taste of his sweat in my mouth.

I make it sound as though it was always glorious, and of course it wasn't always. And I make it sound as though I never loved anyone, and that isn't true either. But that simple contact was also something I loved.

I was in one of those relationships when I met Daniel. The guy's name was Max. He was a bartender at my favorite bar in Honolulu. Diving culture involves a lot of hanging around bars. There are the long, glorious hours you spend underwater and then there are the hours you spend celebrating what you found there or what you did there. Most scientists I've met aren't avid divers. Because I loved it so much, I spent a lot of time with divers and their friends.

Max was Hawaiian. He had long glossy black hair that felt a little bit the way rippling water does over your skin. His body was lean and muscular from surfing and lifting weights, but it was nearly hairless and soft as a child's. He didn't particularly like to talk, which I at first found comforting. I had recently broken up with someone who wanted to do nothing but talk and my ears needed a rest. But after a while, Max's silence started to seem confining.

I met Daniel at a conference—we were on the same panel. The conference had not begun auspiciously. By this point in my career, I was used to my fellow scientists being surprised at me, a youngish black woman, as part of their very white male business. Always, there was the question in the air—*What are* you *doing here?* That day not long before my presentation there was an incident that particularly enraged me. Although there were AV guys at the lecture hall to take care of technical stuff where Daniel and I would be speaking, I was very nervous—it was an important meeting and I wanted to make a good impression. So I got up the morning of the panel, threw on jeans and a T-shirt, and went over to see the space and get comfortable there. I was poking around the back of the stage when a tall, thin white guy came in. I didn't know his name but I'd seen him briefly across the room at the opening night cocktail party. He looked at me quickly, not really seeing me, and then said, without preamble, "Is there any way you can make sure that it isn't too hot in here today? It was broiling at last night's lecture. And there's a garbage can over there that needs to be emptied."

I didn't say anything at first because, frankly, I really didn't understand. But then I did. He thought I was from maintenance. There was no way that someone who looked like *me* could be one of *them,* one of *him,* I guess I should say. "I'm Josephine Henderson, one of the panelists," I said, ice shimmering on every word. He turned the color of a tomato—I didn't think that was actually possible but there it was. Stammering and apologizing and slinking out followed. I sat down alone in the back of the room and took four deep breaths and planted my feet into the floor. I was rooted there. They weren't gonna make me leave.

• • •

A FEW MINUTES BEFORE the panel began, I took my place on stage next to Daniel, and introduced myself briskly. After that morning, I was not feeling all that friendly toward white men. He looked at me in a way that was both oddly preoccupied and curiously penetrating, like he was trying to figure something out important about me. But I wasn't in the mood to look back. The panel started and he went first.

He had a soothing, musical voice. His presentation was fascinating, so much so that without my noticing it my shoulders relaxed and the anger drained out of me enough that I could focus.

We finished our presentations and, as often happened, there were lots of questions for him, none for me. About ten minutes in, an elderly eminence asked Daniel something that pertained directly to warm water mammals, which is what I'd been talking about. His voice was only a little bit tight when he said, "I think that's a question that Dr. Henderson is better prepared to answer. That was, after all, the subject of her talk and she's an expert in that field." Then he turned toward me, smiling a little. I noticed that he had a beautiful smile. And he noticed my skill (and the way some people ignored it) without my having to point it out. I smiled back at him and started to answer the elderly eminence. After that, people started directing questions to us both.

After the panel was over, we stood next to each other, gathering up papers. I spoke first.

"Thanks."

"For what?" He said this while peering into his briefcase and shuffling through it with a distracted air.

"For telling that guy that he should be asking me the questions."

Daniel quit rustling and looked up. "Well, he should have been. You really know your stuff."

"Thanks." I had told Max that I might call him after the panel was over but, suddenly, that didn't seem so important. "Are you doing anything now?"

Again that steady look. "Nope. Are you?"

"I hope I'm having dinner with you." Like some impossibly witty, bold movie heroine. I rarely think of things that clever to say at the time it would be clever to say them.

Daniel smiled broadly. "I didn't expect that." He paused. "But I'd like it. I'd like it a lot." And that's how we had our first date.

You know how people say *I knew right away that he was the one*? It wasn't like that for me. I don't believe in that "the one" stuff anyway. I liked how smart Daniel was. I liked his laugh. I liked that when I told him the story of the trash can, that he was as angry as I was—and he took my hand across the table right afterward. That's where things really began. I broke up with Max, and Daniel and I kept going, slow, smooth, steady, affectionate. Gradually, I moved away from focusing what was on the outside of him—his smile, his body—to take notice of how much he loved me. He told me once that I was the smartest person he'd ever met. He told me once that he dreamed about how I laughed. He told me once that I carried his heart in my back pocket. He doesn't say things like that anymore.

Daniel was a person I could live with, which is also not to be underestimated. I'd been with men who could make me scream with pleasure but whom I couldn't have lived with for more than a week. He was orderly and kind and paid his bills and was respected and respectful. We laughed together. We liked the same movies. We liked to look at each other. He seemed like someone I could spend the rest of my life with. So when he asked me to do that, I said yes.

We were married on a sunny July day when the greenhead flies were biting and the air was fresh and hot and blinding. We were married on a beach near Falmouth. We were married under a big tent that Daniel's mother somehow was able to rent at a discount through a friend of hers. Everyone was willing to help. We were married in our bare feet as the cold waves rolled in and washed over our toes, making them numb and painful. We were married laughing. We were married while everyone we loved watched us. Tick quiet and sober (this was between rehabs) and my mother standing straight and proud beside him and next to my father. My father looked shy and suspicious of the abundance of white people and the cold ocean water and the hot sun. He squinted throughout the ceremony. We were married as Daniel's mother stared at my family, slightly baffled. I don't know if she'd ever seen that many black people together in one place before. And now they were her family. We said we'd always love each other. We said we'd take that leap of faith. Together. I was frightened but it seemed like it was time. He had beautiful hands. I was glad to be marrying those. He was very calm and steady and present. I was glad to be marrying that. He made me feel beautiful. I was glad to be marrying that. What he saw in me. What he made me feel. The way he said my name. The way he looked when he told me about his father's death. That's what I was marrying. That's what I wanted near me. He was the one I wanted.

So here we are. We have a home together. We have a life together. But so often my impulse is to stay away from it. I work late when I don't really have to, take on extra little jobs, have to stay and work just-a-little-bit-longer on that grant or that paper or that observation.

Like last night, a few weeks after I got home from picking up Tick. I came home around ten, exhausted, eyes burning from staring at the computer screen for hours. I'm working on a big study of the effect of LFA (that's low-frequency active) sonar on whales. This is the sonar that navy ships use to track down "quiet" submarines—it blasts low frequency sound waves for hundreds of miles under the sea. On the way to the submarines, it impairs all the sentient marine life it encounters. The blasts of sound disorient and disable their delicate internal mechanisms and their hearing. Just another way that humans are making it rough, rough, rough for every other life form on this planet. It's depressing.

Anyway, I came home late and miserable. The lights were out already. I wandered around the kitchen, eating random foods, turned on the TV for a few minutes to watch a rerun of something or other, then went up to bed.

"You're awfully late," Daniel said as soon as I lay down. I sighed.

"Yeah, I was working on this study—you know. Wanted to get a little ahead if I could."

"Oh." Something about the way he said that didn't sound good.

"Is something wrong?" I asked.

"I just wish . . ." he paused. "I wish you were home for dinner a little more often—we only manage maybe two or three times a week." He laughed a little. "I thought the man was the one who was supposed to flee domestic life."

"Well, Daniel, you've always known this about me. That I work a lot. I always have. And this study is due soon." I took a deep breath and tried to push the edge out of my voice. "I love you but I've gotta do my work. You know that."

"I know. I have work to do, too. But I try to be here when I can. I'm willing to make a family. To make this our home."

I didn't say anything. Just looked up at the ceiling in the dark. I knew I should turn toward him and embrace him. Tell him I loved him and loved our home. But I didn't move. Something seemed to be pinning my arms to the familiar sheets. "Aren't you going to say anything?" he said after a while.

"I'm not sure what to say. I love you, Danny. I just had to finish this thing."

"Okay." He sighed. "I'm going to sleep now." He pushed up on his elbow to kiss me. He rolled over and drifted off. I stared at the ceiling, wishing I was anywhere but there.

THE NEXT DAY WAS Friday. We had been invited to a party that evening at my boss Bill Hanna's house. It was being held in honor of a new colleague, Benjamin Davidson. When we got the Evite, I forwarded it to Daniel with a note on the top that said: "Sigh. I guess we've got to make an appearance at this thing." He sent back a little sad face, but there was no getting out of it.

Bill Hanna was the only one of our colleagues that I truly disliked. He was the director of the Marine Biology Department so he was my boss, which made it even more unpleasant. He had a booming, unmodulated voice and he usually smelled slightly of onions. Here's the kind of guy he was: He'd have twenty people over and maybe two bowls of chips. Not only was this annoying, but people got drunk at his parties because there wasn't enough to eat. I really hated that.

Daniel and I sat at breakfast with our respective cups of coffee, not talking much, which we usually don't in the morning. I was the first to speak. "So I'm sorry about last night, Danny. I think you're right. I mean, I can try to be home a little bit more. I just lose track of time. But you're important to me, too. Really." I reached across the table and took his hand. He squeezed back and smiled a little but didn't speak. "Let's have dinner tonight before Bill's, okay? We're gonna need something to eat anyway—you know how he is. There won't even kind of be enough food." That made Daniel laugh, and my heart contracted with pleasure and virtue. How could I lose sight of him so easily? He was such a dear, good man. What could I have been thinking? I got up to go get dressed for work and stopped to kiss him like I meant it, another thing that I don't do enough. He slapped my butt as I left the kitchen to go get ready for the day. I sang off-key in the shower.

My good mood and good intentions continued all day; I worked like a demon, and Daniel and I had a lovely dinner. We held hands as we walked over to Bill's.

"Hey, how the hell are you!" boomed Bill as he opened the door.

My voice instantly got small and mouselike. How could I find someone so annoying and so intimidating at the same time? "We're good, Bill. How about you?" I pecked his cheek and Daniel shook his hand. "Good to have you back, Josie. How was your trip home? Everything okay?"

I hadn't said anything specific to anyone at work about why I'd gone home. Truth be told, I'd barely talked about it with Daniel. It made me too uncomfortable—and of course there was that little nibble of shame. I'd made good—why couldn't my brother get it together? And a fearful step further: My foothold in this world is tenuous enough—I don't need them to think I fit the stereotype of black girl with a no 'count brother. I've had only one friend who has lived with that shaming cruel fear the way I have: my college roommate Maren. I still talk to her every so often, even though I live across the country now—we used to be tighter than tight. Like me, she finished Stanford with honors, but she went on to law school and then got a job at one of the leading law firms in L.A. She never looked less than perfect and she rose through the firm like a rocket. But there was someone just behind her, hidden in her blinding glow.

Periodically, in her vast shining office with a view, she would have to field panicked calls from her brother on his way back to jail for the third or fourth or who-knows-how-many times on some petty drug bust. Sometimes she'd bring her legal expertise into play to help him—but she did it on the sly. "I always have to close the door for those calls," she told me once as we sat under umbrellas at a café on Melrose, sipping tall, cool green drinks. "I can't help him anymore and I can't let them know at the firm that I'm related to somebody like that. What am I gonna say? What are they going to think of me?" She laughed bitterly. "If I get this associate's job at Kelley and Thompson, I'm not giving him my work number. I can't." I nodded—I knew exactly what she meant. There was the worry and love for your brother along with the embarrassment and shame with yourself for being embarrassed. It was toxic, but we shared it. I told her about Tick. She understood. But now? Now there was no one in my professional life that I felt safe telling, Bill Hanna least of all. So I put on a big smile and said, "Oh, fine, fine. It was no big deal. Everyone's fine."

"Good, good." He wasn't listening anyway—it didn't matter what I said. "Well, come on in and drop your stuff and then meet the newest member of our department."

Scientist parties are more raucous than cliché would have you believe. It is true that many of us are more comfortable with objects than people, but we like to drink beer and gossip about our peers and dance awkwardly to the hit records of our youth as much as any other group of professionals. Daniel went off to get us both drinks after we deposited our stuff. That's when I saw Ben.

I couldn't help but see him. He and I were the only black people in the room. He was standing alone, holding a guacamole-covered chip. I went right over to him.

"So, welcome to Woods Hole."

He shoved his chip into his mouth quickly and stuck his hand out. "Hi, I'm Ben Davidson."

"Josie Henderson."

He had a firm, dry grip and very direct brown eyes. "I wasn't sure if I'd be the only one."

"Well, I've been the only for a while but yeah, now we're taking over."

He grinned. "Taking over Woods Hole. Yeah. Black Power."

We smiled at each other wordlessly for a minute. Then Daniel came over with our beers and Ben's girlfriend, Leslie, came out of the bathroom (a thin blonde with red-framed glasses) and we did introductions all around and started talking about the department and life in Woods Hole and so on.

It was easy to stand there. Daniel would occasionally touch the small of my back as if to make sure I was still with him. Ben was funny and almost unnervingly smart, opinions and remarks and questions flying out of him like bullets. I gave as good as I got. Leslie didn't talk much but she smiled at what we had to say. I had one more beer than I usually do and I had a really good time, laughing and hugging Daniel exuberantly and talking very loudly and once or twice touching Ben on the shoulder to make a point. After a while, I didn't even mind that there were only Doritos. I ate a lot of them. Suddenly, I was starving.

I WORK IN THE newer building at Woods Hole—it's called the Marine Research Facility and it's on a back road about two miles outside of the center of town. In many ways, the town grew up around the old building, which has been there since the 1930s. Daniel works there as well. It's big, constructed in old red brick, and covered with ivy—it looks like some of the old schools in Cleveland. The research facility is just off a beautiful bike path between Falmouth and Woods Hole. I love to ride it, but because I work late so often, I don't ride as much as I'd like. I don't like to bike around the Hole at night. There's no crime to speak of, but it's pitch dark along the bike path. The city girl in me still hates the absolute dark of a country night.

Anyway, it was a perfect day for a ride. I was cruising along, thinking of nothing in particular, when I heard someone pedaling up on my right. "Hey." I swerved a little, startled. It was Ben. He had mentioned at the party that he was going to be working in the same building I did.

"Hey, Ben. On your way to work? You and Leslie don't live over here, do you?"

"No, no, we live across the canal. But I love to ride, so I drive over the bridge and try to squeeze in a little whenever I can."

"I know, it's nice, right? I feel so lucky to live in a place like this. Seeing the ocean every day."

"I know. Back home . . . well, it wasn't much like this back home."

"Are you from Miami originally?"

"Nah. Hardly anybody's from Miami originally. Hardly anybody black anyway. I'm from Detroit."

I squealed, a lot more girlishly than I usually do. "Hey, I'm from Cleveland! Struggling midwestern towns unite!"

We'd made it up the hill now and laughed as we locked our bikes to the rack. "Struggling midwestern towns unite," he said. "Sad but true. Did you grow up in the city?"

"Born and raised. My parents still live there."

"Me too. Me too." He turned toward the building. "You going in?"

"Of course."

"Then after you."

"Where's your office?" I asked, once we'd gotten inside.

"Hmm." He looked down at his iPhone. "Supposed to be number 195."

"Hey, that's right next to me—it's been empty for a while. It'll be nice to have a neighbor." He didn't say anything. But he smiled at me in a way that made my toes curl up inside my shoes. I looked away for a minute. When I looked back, he was still gazing at me, a ghost of that smile on his face. "Well," I said, "well, good luck getting settled. We should get to work."

"Right," he said. And then he turned and unlocked his office door and went in. I stood in front of my door for a second and then let myself in. My hands shook a little. I started working—but I could hear him moving around through the wall, blinds going up and down, an occasional cough.

After that, we were friendly to each other in the halls

and we had lunch together a few times—lunches at which I was careful to mention Daniel frequently and refrain from any physical contact. I have to admit, I liked seeing his dark face around. He wasn't a knockout in the traditional sense. But he had clear, dark eyes that always seemed to really *see* me and a pretty, generous mouth. He wore sort of Buddy Holly–looking glasses that somehow suited his narrow face. But I told myself that noticing all this was just how it was—I was married, not dead. No harm in noticing an attractive man.

After Ben had been working at the institute for about three weeks, we both ended up going out on the *Tioga* (that's the institute's research vessel—it's fantastic). For the first time in a while, some of the whales we had been tracking had come in close enough for us to observe them. We also needed to check up on some of the equipment we keep way offshore to monitor water conditions and such. I was glad to have the chance to get out of the office. It had been months since I'd been in the water and I was still on edge from my time in Cleveland, even though I'd only exchanged a few desultory texts with Tick. I'd been especially restless for the last couple of weeks, spinning in my office chair and playing desktop solitaire when I was supposed to be working.

The first time Ben and I ever discussed diving, not long after he started at the institute, I knew right away that he loved diving the way I did, another thing about him that I noted with pleasure. I was looking forward to seeing him in the water. We sat next to each other in the van that drove us out to the launch, not saying much. Our legs were almost, almost touching, so close that I could feel the heat of his skin. But we didn't talk about that. We just sat that way until we arrived and then hopped out of the van together and went over to the dock. But my chest felt a little tight, my stomach a little jumpy. I don't usually get nervous before a dive—it was odd.

I always get a kick out of seeing other divers' faces when they first catch sight of the *Tioga*. After he got his first good look at it, I could hear his short intake of breath—"Wow," he said, "What a beautiful boat."

I smiled.

"I know, isn't it? Sometimes I think I should pay them for getting to go out on it. Come on—let me show you."

We hopped on deck and I showed him all around as we pushed off—he oohed and ahhed and said "oh man, that's great" at everything.

"This is the best research boat I've ever seen. I can't believe it. I can't believe I get to work here."

Finally I said, "Yeah, I can't believe it either."

After a while we got far enough out that we began to see whales in the distance and everything else was forgotten in the need to get to work and the never-diminishing thrill of seeing the whales. The captain said he was going to turn us about and that we'd better get ready if we wanted to get in the water today.

I was doing everything you always have to do—spitting in my mask, checking levels on my tank, making sure there were no holes in the equipment. Then I looked up and caught sight of Ben. He was similarly preoccupied, his head turned a little away from me, his wet suit pulled up over his legs but not yet all the way on. He was positioned so that the sun was behind him. It outlined his dark brown body and the back of his neck and suddenly it was like I'd been hit from behind. I understood my antsiness, my nervousness, everything. He didn't look at me. But I suddenly wanted him to. I cared whether or not he did. I was glad Daniel wasn't with us.

We went in together. Though I do love the whales, I've never liked the diving here as much as I liked warm-water diving. But that day was different: I loved it. Ben was a beautiful diver, moving so economically that he might have been part fish himself. The water pushed against my legs as hard as a lover, and I kicked and eased my way through it like it was where I belonged. It was where we both belonged. The sound of my breath amplified by the mouthpiece went in and out of my ears glassily. Once or twice I felt as though I could hear him breathing, too. We did the work we needed to do in sync, as though we'd been diving together forever. We came out of the water at the same time, hauled up on deck, and half-stripped. We sat next to each other, not talking. He was the first one to speak. "A bunch of us are going out to the Captain Kidd tonight. You'll come with us, right?"

"Wouldn't miss it."

"Good."

YOU HAVE ALL THIS energy after a good dive—it's like you've left planet Earth and come back. It's weird to be breathing and not to hear your own breath, the way you do underwater. If you hold your breath while you're diving, you can throw an air embolus or your lungs might collapse. Diving instructors have two approaches to teaching students this information: They either soft-pedal it, stressing that it's important but not being explicit, or they delight in the horror-show aspect of it, putting the fear of God into you so completely that you never, ever quit thinking of your lungs while you're diving for the first few times. My instructor was one of the latter types. He scared me so badly that I could hardly pay attention to what was around me my first few dives. But then I started being unable to resist the beauty all around me and I started breathing more evenly and it was all right.

So that's how I was feeling once we got showered and back on land. It was around sixty-thirty or so. I called Daniel to see if he wanted to come, but even as I did it, I knew he wouldn't—he hates bars, and he wasn't all buzzed up the way I was. Is it terrible to say that I was glad he didn't come? Well, I was. There was a whole gang of us, my friend Sally Tobias from the Geology Department and Ben and about six other people. Only four of us had been on the dive—everyone else just wanted a drink. So off we went to the Captain Kidd, which has very good cheeseburgers and a vast array of beers. It doesn't look much different from any other bar you can think of: neon, the smell of booze, grit underfoot, graffiti in the bathroom. It's close to the bay, which is nice. If you step out to get some air, you can see the water. Anyway, there we were. I was sitting with my friend Sally and we were talking about . . . work? Not work? Something we read online? I can't remember. But here's what I remember: Out of the corner of my eye, I saw Ben get up and go to the jukebox and incline his head toward it to pick a song. His neck had a kind of precise curve, as though it had been carefully sculpted by a loving hand. The blue light of the jukebox reflected off his glasses and gave his face a bluish glow. His hands tapped the side of the juke, and I stared at them as if they would explain what was happening. Sally was still talking. I kept nodding, not hearing. He punched some buttons and then his song came on: Prince's version of "Nothing Compares 2 U." I couldn't believe that song was on the jukebox, let alone that Ben had picked it—most people only know Sinead O'Connor's version, even though Prince wrote it. His version of it is on his greatest-hits album. The music vibrated through me as Ben walked away from the bar. I kept looking at him and I could feel, in the palms of my hands, every part of his body. I know this sounds silly. But it's what happened. I watched him the rest of the night. I said a few things to him at one point—something about how I loved that song. And he said "Yeah, I love it, too. You know how sometimes a song comes on and you know you'll never forget it. It just gets you at the right moment." And I said "yeah" and my heart was slamming under my ribs. Prince washed over us both like a benediction. Someone called Ben's name and he turned away to answer. He talked a lot to everybody. He threw his head back when he laughed. His whole body got involved; he even slapped the table once. I thought about resting my mouth on one of his earlobes. His hand wrapped around his beer bottle was the most interesting hand I'd ever seen. He looked at me once and his eyes got still. But then he went back to talking and laughing and I thought maybe I made it up. As I drove home I imagined sitting with him in a coffee shop sometime, holding hands and gazing at each other very steadily, not talking.

After that, working with him was different, for all that it was the same. We didn't have the same specialty but sometimes we had to collaborate. A few times, he came into my office and leaned over my computer to show me something in one of his reports and his arm brushed near my chest as he slid the mouse around and I knew. At that moment, I knew that this feeling I was having was not under my control. I was going to have it until I stopped having it, no matter how much sorrow and trouble it might cause.

What am I supposed to do with this? I'm married. I'm a married woman now. A married woman in her thirties. I'm not allowed to slide my hands down his shoulders, feel his skin next to mine, hear what kinds of sounds he'd make, feel his breath in my ear, look into his eyes, taste his sweat, feel that kinky hair under my hands after so many years of straight hair, after so many years of the same body, after so many years of the same man. I can't do that. I chose Daniel. I said I'd have him forever.

Sometimes when I wake up, I know I've dreamed about making love to Ben. Sometimes when I make love to my husband, I say Ben's name into the pillow, over and over, a chant, a dream, a wish. I don't tell anyone this. But I know it.

Fourteen

A month or so after Tick got home from Riverrun, reports from my mother were brief but mostly good news—or at least not bad news. He was going to work every day and a meeting almost every night.

One morning I was looking at a picture of us that I kept on my bureau. We were only about eight and six in the photo, out in front of our house. I was holding a bucket and standing a little bit behind him, smiling. He was astride one of those sticks with a stuffed horse head, charging straight toward the camera, ready for anything. He looked like he could take on the world. I jumped when my cell phone rang, picked up without looking at the number.

"Hey, Josie. It's Tick."

"Whoa. Hey Tick. This is so weird. I was just looking at that old picture. You know the one where you're riding Black Lightning?"

He laughed. He sounded like himself. The self he was at his best. "Man, I loved that horse. He was the greatest."

I laughed, too. "How are you, Tick?" Maybe it was looking at the photo. Maybe it was his laugh. Maybe it was knowing that I should give him more than I do. But I willed some kindness, some openness into my heart, into my voice.

"I'm all right. Doing all right. Work's good. Ain't the same since LeBron left but, you know. At least all the craziness is over."

"I know! People lost their minds over that stuff. For God's sake, the guy's allowed to work someplace else if he wants to."

Tick laughed again. "Players don't really think of it as working someplace else, Josie. People who talk about themselves in the third person—well, they're a little different from you and me."

"Right." A friendly silence between us.

"Well, Josie, I know you got to get to work. I need to leave, too. I just wanted to say hey. And say . . . say that I'm doing okay. I'm keeping clean, going to meetings. I'm doing okay."

My hand was tight on the phone, my voice almost a

whisper when I said, "That's great, Tick. That's really great. I'm so happy to hear it."

"All right. Call me, okay? Or at least answer a brother's texts, okay?"

"Okay . . . you punk."

"Who you calling a punk?" he said. It was our old loving tease. "I'll talk to you later, Josie-face."

"Later Tick-tock."

I was alone in the house. It took me ten minutes to get myself together enough to leave for work. My baby brother. How I loved him.

FOR OUR PART, Daniel and I kept to our routines—which included unprotected sex. We reached an uneasy détente about my getting pregnant: We didn't use birth control but I wouldn't take things any further—no ovulation watching, no sperm checks, no IVF (which we couldn't afford anyway), none of that. Every month when my period came, I felt as though I'd gotten away with something. Daniel looked so disappointed, and for his sake, I wished I felt the same. But I was happy to see the blood on the tissue, an old friend that meant I was not going to be a mother. We didn't talk about what was going on, but it grew—silent and hulking.

One Sunday morning, a springtime morning, we were

avoiding talking by both being deeply immersed in the *New York Times.* I'm a real old fogy about it—most of my colleagues wouldn't dream of reading the newspaper anywhere but on their laptops, but I like to sit with a cup of coffee and spread the whole thing around me in inky, tree-killing profusion. Reading the paper is one of the few things I can remember my parents doing together—sitting in companionable silence, my mother drinking coffee. Daniel has the same old-fashioned bias, so we subscribe—it costs a fortune, but we agreed it was a necessary indulgence. I was lying on the sofa with the "Week in Review," and Daniel was in his favorite easy chair across from me scowling through an article in the business section. Our cat, Samantha, was asleep between my legs. The warmth there was soothing and vaguely sexual, but not a feeling I was particularly inclined to do anything about at that moment. I was deep into a piece about a cloning scandal when the phone rang. I'm the one who answers the phone around here. People rarely call for Daniel. He's a solitary soul. He has colleagues—but not friends who might call on a Sunday morning. He seems to feel that knowing that the phone is not for him exempts him from needing to respond to that particular sound. I sighed, pushed Samantha off me, and got up.

"Hello?"

"Hi, it's me."

I walked into the other room with the phone. "Ben? Hi. What is it?" Since that night at the bar, we had begun to lunch together more often. When we sat together in the cafeteria or at one or the other of our cramped desks, our knees not quite touching.

"What are you doing?"

"I was sitting on the sofa, reading the paper with Daniel. We're just hanging out. What's going on? Are you okay?"

He paused for a long time. "It's about Leslie. Josie, she moved out today. All her things are gone, she packed everything. She's going back to Florida."

I'd met Ben's girlfriend but he didn't talk about her much. He never said, "Well, we . . ." or "The other day Leslie said . . ." I'd noticed this and, in my more fevered moments, wondered if it had something to do with me. My Daniel mentions, at first quite frequent, had gone way down since that night in the bar. Even so, I was a little surprised that I was the one Ben would call at a moment like this. I was also a little pleased.

"Ben, you're kidding. Really? I'm so sorry."

"Listen, I know we don't usually talk on the weekends, but do you think you could get away today and meet me?"

"We don't have anything planned. Yeah. Sure."

"OK. Can you meet me at the beach over in Falmouth, maybe around noon? I want to be by the water today."

"Sure. Absolutely. Around noon. Do you want to have lunch?"

"Why don't you have lunch first? I'm not hungry anyway. I was up all night, trying to talk to her. I don't want to eat."

"Okay. I'll see you in a little while, then."

"Thanks, Josie."

I went back to the living room. My Sunday-morning calm had vanished—I felt keyed-up, shiny. Daniel looked up from the sports section. "Who was that?"

"Ben."

"Ah."

"What's that supposed to mean?"

"What's what supposed to mean?"

" 'Ah.' He's my friend. Can't a friend call?"

Daniel lowered the paper and looked at me evenly. "Of course a friend can call."

A band tightened around my head. I sat back down on the sofa and rested my hand on Daniel's foot. "Sorry. He's upset. His girlfriend moved out."

Daniel wiggled his toes under my hand. "That's too bad."

"Yeah. He asked me to meet him later."

"Well, that's okay. I was going to go to the lab anyway. That way you'll have something to do."

"I'd have something to do anyway." Again, that same sharp tone in my voice.

"I know that." The same mildness in his.

Daniel's dissertation was about the coelacanth, which seems somehow appropriate. These fish were assumed to be extinct until 1938, when a fisherman caught one off the coast of South Africa. Since then, they've popped up every so often, there and in the deepest waters off Indonesia. They are rare and big and quiet and slow-moving. They keep to themselves and move at great depths. Though my expertise is in warm-water mammals, my favorite fish are the tropical ones, even though I'm stuck up here in the cold water. I suppose that's a difference between us. I like bright things that flit about. He likes things to be even and predictable. I am much less sure of the value of that. That steadiness was one of the first things I liked about him. But now sometimes I wish he'd get a little crazy. I couldn't sit still suddenly. I went out to the porch to breathe.

Our house always smells slightly of the sea—I'm so grateful we're not far from the ocean. But as I stood out on the porch breathing in that fresh-washed air, I wished I could have just one more cig. Just a moment when that smoke eased into my lungs and quieted everything. I quit not long after Daniel and I started going out. Of course I knew how bad it was for me. Of course I knew the danger. I spend a lot of my time around oxygen tanks and a lot of my time underwater. I know that your lungs are important.

But I started in college. I liked the way it looked. I liked, for once, doing something I wasn't supposed to. And then, of course, I wanted to stop and I couldn't. That's addiction for you. It took me three tries before I was truly able to give it up. It was starting to affect my breathing on dives; that's what finally made me do it. I wouldn't mess that up for anything.

I crossed my arms and took a deep breath. Daniel put some music on inside the house. "Smells Like Teen Spirit." He has a soft spot for Nirvana—perhaps it's that wildness in them. I don't like them that much. The way all Kurt Cobain's pain is just out there—it scares me. I sighed and looked up at the sky. It was a perfect angel blue day. I squeezed my upper arms briefly and then went back inside to decide what to wear. I tried to think of something pretty that wouldn't be so dressed up that Daniel would wonder why I was making an effort. He didn't look up as I walked past him. One of his feet was moving in time to the music.

I MET BEN IN the parking lot at Stony Beach. He had gotten out of his car and was leaning against the hood, looking around for me. I sat in the car for a minute, gazing at him. He really wasn't so spectacular—he looked a little owlish behind his black-framed glasses, and he was too thin. But he was such a lovely color, and his mouth was so sweet and curved. What I liked best about him was his eyes—when I looked at him, I could see that someone was fully alive in there. Very sexy. I sighed and got out of the car and waved as I walked toward him.

He pushed off the hood and took a few steps toward me. As I reached him, he hugged me, which I did not expect. It went right through to my toes. "I'm so glad to see you. Thanks for coming," he said. We both leaned awkwardly back against the hood. I slid my hand lightly and quickly across his back, over his cotton T-shirt.

"Sure, Ben. What happened?"

"She's gone. We had a really big fight last night and she just packed her bag and left. She went to her sister's in Boston."

"Have you guys been fighting a lot?"

He had been looking at the ground in front of him but now he looked up, dead into my eyes. My hand was still on his back. "We have. She couldn't get a decent gig here and I've been kind of distracted."

"By what?"

"I think you know." He pushed off the car. "Let's walk, okay?"

As we moved away from the car, he gently took my hand. Just as gently, I didn't pull away. We walked out with all the beach-going families, hand in hand like any couple anywhere. We found a quiet place and let go of each other's hands, spread out a blanket, sat down, talked. I don't remember much of what he said. I remember certain gestures he made—a smile, the way he reached off the blanket with his toes and dug in the sand. He didn't say anything flirtatious or anything about me or us at all. He talked about Leslie, what might have gone wrong, what he might do now. Neither of us said anything about taking the other's hand. Neither of us said anything about there even *being* an us. Better to talk about the woman who was gone than about the man and woman who sat across from each other, thinking so much more than they were saying. We sat and talked for an hour or two. He walked me back to my car and after I opened the door and sat down I looked up and said, "I'm glad you called me. Hope I helped."

"Just being around you helps." He touched my cheek so lightly that I might have imagined it. Then he turned and walked away.

My mother called about a week or so later.

"Hi, Mom."

"Hey, baby. How are you?"

"Okay, I guess. Just sitting here working on a grant." The game of desktop solitaire I had been playing seemed to blink at me, as if surprised by the boldness of my lie.

"Well, that's good. Is it hot there?"

"Not too. You know it doesn't get real hot up here until July. It's all right." She didn't say anything, so I kept talking about nothing important. "How is it there?"

"Oh, you know. Kind of muggy. The trees help—it doesn't ever get too hot in the house." She paused again. "So."

"Mom, what's going on?"

"It's Tick." Tick. Tick again. Always Tick. When he was a kid, this is the kind of thing people used to say about him: *Shame having those eyelashes on a boy.*

Mmm-hmm. And that good hair.

I'm telling you, Sarah. You better be ready when that boy gets bigger and the girls start coming around. It's gonna be like I don't know what. But I know you better get ready, girl.

I suppose I should say that they never said that kind of stuff about me. I was the smart one. I was pretty enough for all general purposes. Fix me up and I looked all right—Tick and I look something alike. But I could never quite get myself to care about it sufficiently. And I would have had to. I would have had to put in some effort to have what he had when he rolled out of bed in the morning.

You should have seen him in high school. I would walk past him at his locker and some girl would be talking to him and I could tell by the set of her head and the intentness of her gaze that she couldn't have cared less about whatever they were talking about. She just wanted to see what his lips looked like as he spoke. She just wanted to soak up a little of the stardust that flaked off him as he moved to put his books in his locker.

Imagine if that were your brother. I used to look at myself in the mirror and wonder why things hadn't fallen quite the same way on my face as they had on his. I used to watch everyone jostling to be near him and feel my heart twist in my chest. Then other times, that twisting would fall away. I would sit in the stands at basketball games and watch him run and feel so proud and full of joy. I hoped everyone could see that he was my baby brother.

Well. People don't say that kind of stuff about him anymore. No point in saying that. I was silent. My mother was silent. Finally, we both started to speak at the same time, our tired, anxious voices running into each other. I won out. "What's going on, Mom?"

"I don't know. He's going to work and going to meetings right along, just like he's supposed to. But he seems kind of jumpy. I don't know. He's just either in the basement by himself or at a meeting. I don't know how that can be all he wants to do."

"He's not using, though, is he, Mom?"

"No, no, I don't think so. I'm just always worried that he'll start again."

"Well, you'll know if he does, right?"

A long silence. Then, "Yes. Yes, I will."

"Mom?"

"Yeah?"

"Do you have anyone that you talk to about all this? Maybe you should think about going to some of those meetings."

"Okay, baby, I will. . . . I should go. I'm sure you have things to do." That was that. Every time anyone mentions meetings, she shuts down.

My mother refuses to go to Al-Anon, even though she's had to deal with not one but two alcoholics for so many years. I have no idea why. Well. Yes, I do. She's ashamed still, and embarrassed that both her husband and her son have walked the same dark road. I shouldn't talk. I'm the same way—but for her it's different. That's her ex-husband, her child. She seems closer somehow—maybe it'd help her. Maybe it'd give her something to lean on besides my resistant shoulders. She has to deal with Tick all the time. That's what those twelve-step programs are for, right? For people who have to deal with that shit all the time. I haven't truly dealt with Tick in years. I picked him up from Riverrun because my mother begged me to. But since then? I'm done. I'm not going down with him. I'm not.

I turned my chair around so I could look out the window for a minute. My chest hurt and my eyes stung. I got up and went next door to Ben's office.

He opened the door quickly at my knock. Unlike me, he had clearly actually been working on something or other. He looked preoccupied. Until he saw it was me.

"Hey, Josie, come on in. Hi." He quickly lifted some papers up off a chair—his office was an insane mess. Unlike Daniel's, in which it is hard to find a paper clip unless you know which drawer they are kept in. The neatness is absolute, unapproachable. There is never even any dust or coffee cup rings on Daniel's desk; he goes over it with a Swiffer cloth every morning.

"Hi, Ben." I sat down.

"What's up?"

"Oh, I don't know. Having trouble focusing this morning. My mother called. You know."

He sat back down on his side of the desk. He looked right at me. "Something wrong at home?"

I hadn't told him about Tick. About all the back and forth, the drugs and the booze, the in and out of rehab.

"Maybe," I said.

He looked at me some more. "It's my brother," I said.

"Yeah?"

"Yeah. He still lives in Cleveland. His name's Tick." I hesitated, biting my lip. I was thinking, *I don't want to talk about this I don't want to talk about this,* but at the same time, I wanted to trust him. I knew I could trust him.

"So what's going on?"

I looked at the wall behind his head. He had hung up some pictures—a cartoon from the *New Yorker,* a still of Jerry Lewis in a lab coat from *The Nutty Professor.* I took a deep breath. "Tick's an amazing guy. Funny, good-looking, charming. I'd probably want to date him if he weren't my brother. He kind of glows. He's always been like that.

"But for the last, I don't know, ten years, he's been drunk. Or high. Or both. I don't even know what all on. It's always something. He's been in and out of rehab twice. I had to go home to help my parents and pick him up from rehab right before you moved here. Sometimes he's all speedy—I mean faster than normal speedy. But mostly he's just drunk. Not so drunk he can't keep a job for a while anyway. But then he fucks up. He works as a trainer with the Cleveland Cavs, and he's almost lost that job. He's sober for now. My mother's still trying to save him. But I don't know if she can. I don't know if anyone can."

"Why don't you think he'll stay sober?" he asked.

"I don't know. Did I say I didn't think he'd stay sober? I think he will. I mean . . . I don't know what he'll do. I want him to stay sober. It's up to him, I guess."

Ben looked at me hard. "Why'd you come talk to me about it?"

I looked back at him. "I like talking to you. Why'd you call me when Leslie left?"

Ben came around the desk and kind of lifted me into his arms. I fit perfectly. "I like talking to you, too." I didn't move away from him. I could feel his hand moving in little circles on my back. He was hesitant at first, just kissed me very gently. But when I opened my mouth just the littlest bit, inviting him, we started kissing the way I'd imagined so often. I felt like a person in a desert having her first drink of water at the end of a long, long day. I thought of my first dive. The way I wished I could somehow live like that, underwater, at home. I didn't think of Daniel. Not for one single solitary second. It was as if he'd never existed at all.

After a while, we stepped apart. The office was very quiet. We stood in each other's arms, breathing in each other's skin. "I'm sorry," he whispered, in my ear, mournful.

I pulled back far enough that he could see that I meant what I was about to say. "I'm not," I said. "I will never be sorry." I didn't know what was going to happen next. But I knew what I said was the truth. "I'd better go." I wiped at my eyes and my mouth with the back of my hand. I just wanted to kiss him again.

"I'll talk with you later," I said.

"Sure. Later."

I turned and left the room without looking back. I'll never know how I managed that. Once I was out the door, I went back to my office in a daze. I went in. Sat down. Gazed absently at the wall. The kiss wasn't the start of this thing. It wasn't the middle, or the end. It ratified what was already happening. I didn't know what I would do. I didn't know what I was capable of anymore.

NOTHING HAD CHANGED and everything had changed. I worked better than I had in months on my grant, suddenly inspired; it was obvious what needed to be said to earn that money. I deserved it. My scholarship was impeccable. I knew exactly what to write. Every now and then, I would look up from the screen and stretch my arms and the whole thing would suddenly be back, right *in* my body. I was kissing Ben again. We were kissing and we weren't going to stop. Who cared about plankton and how they were affected by the warming of the ocean? Who cared about fish? His tongue was in my mouth. We were almost the same color, the same small round heads, dark brown with closely cropped hair. Who cared about the fate of the earth? Not me. He was the only thing I cared about. He satisfied my mind.

BEFORE EVERYTHING CHANGED, part of my new, be-home, be-present promise to myself about Daniel was that I made a point of cooking dinner a couple of times a week. It kind of broke my heart how much it pleased him. And I liked being there to cook for us. I do love him. That was the funny thing about my feelings for Ben—in most ways, they had nothing to do with Daniel. My feelings for them seemed like two entirely separate but necessary chambers of my heart. I got home, went upstairs, changed into stretchy clothes, and put on an old Rufus CD that I hadn't played in years; Rufus was before my time, but they are so great. "Sweet Thing"—what a song. I was fooling around in the kitchen with the salmon and just chiming in with Chaka on the high part—"Love me now or I'll go crazy"—when Daniel came in. He stuck his head in the kitchen.

"What are you making?"

"Salmon."

"Hope it's not farmed."

"You know I don't buy farmed salmon." He started nodding his head to the music. "What is this?"

"What's what?" I'd turned back to the stove, my hips swaying a little.

"This music. It's good."

"You don't know who this is?"

Daniel's eyebrows went up at my tone. He looked as though he had just realized that he'd filled in the wrong bubble on an important standardized test. "No, I don't."

"It's Rufus. Chaka Khan and Rufus. From the seventies. I used to hear it all the time on the oldies stations when I was a kid." Chaka wailed in the background. "Dinner will be ready soon. Why don't you go on up and get changed." Daniel hated to eat dinner in his work clothes, even though his work clothes were jeans and a polo shirt. He'd wear shorts all year if he could.

What kind of a person doesn't recognize "Sweet Thing" as soon as he hears that unforgettable voice? A person who grew up in a very different world from me, that's what kind of person. A person whose porch didn't face out onto a little blacktop street when he was growing up and who never heard a car go by with Earth, Wind & Fire or Rufus pounding out of the window, a cup of warm Kool-Aid at his feet and the music sliding under his skin. Daniel didn't know about that. Ben did.

I am not particularly hung up on race. I've dated all kinds of guys. But when I thought about Ben touching me, I thought, too, about the way in which we were the same color, or at least close in color. I thought about how he knew some things I knew without my having to explain them. I hadn't been aware of missing that until now. Another thing Ben woke up in me.

The salmon was done. I called Daniel to dinner.

He sat down and didn't say anything. He had a slightly wounded look that made my heart contract a bit. Why was I treating him so badly? He couldn't help being who he was or having grown up where he grew up any more than I could. He was so kind to me. How could I be angry at him for that? What was I doing? I reached across the table and took his hand. "Sorry. It was kind of a rough day at work." A lie. A lie to apologize.

"Okay." He was quiet a moment. "I liked that CD."

"Thanks. It's one of my favorites from when I was younger."

He squeezed my hand and pulled away to pick up his fork. "So what happened today at work?"

Here is an astonishment. I started talking about my grant

as though it was just another night. As though it had been just another day. As I talked, it started to feel like just another night. Me and my husband, sitting at the table, talking. For a little while, I forgot Ben's lips on mine. Maybe I could have them both, maybe I could manage this whole thing without any injury. For a little while that night, it felt like I could.

The next day, Ben was standing by my office door when I arrived. Have you ever had all the breath leave your body at once? It's a very interesting feeling. Makes it hard to stand up. My hands shook so hard manipulating the keys that I could barely get the door open. He didn't say anything until we were inside. I went behind my desk. He didn't follow me. He stood very deliberately on the other side and he didn't sit down, even when I gestured that he should. "Josie," he said then. Just my name. "How are you?"

"How am I?" I laughed a little. "I'm preoccupied. How are you?"

"The same."

He looked at me for a minute. A thousand things went through his eyes. But he didn't say any of them. He pressed his beautiful hands together. I looked at them. He sighed. "I'd better go," he said. He had his hand on the knob, his back to me, when he said, "I'll see you for lunch, right?" His voice hopeful.

My heart sang. "Same time as always." I wondered if he could hear the singing in my voice. He wasn't as strong as he was trying to be. I was glad of that.

LUNCH WAS PRETTY MUCH like it always was. I had a salad. Ben had a turkey sandwich. We talked about work, about a lecture we'd gone to the previous week. It was as if that kiss hadn't happened. Or as if we might indeed sail right past it. But then he said, "Anything to say about yesterday?"

"You mean, about what happened in your office?"

"Yeah. I mean what happened in my office."

I looked away from him. "I don't know. It shouldn't happen again." I said.

"No. Probably not."

Even as I said this, I wanted to slide next to him and lay my head on his chest and feel his lips pressing against my skull.

Ben looked at me for a moment, then away. "Well. What about your brother, then?"

"That's a switch."

"Not sure what else to say about . . . well, you know. So what about your brother?"

I twisted my fingers together so hard that they hurt a little. "What about him?"

"Why don't you tell me a little more about him? What's happened before?"

I could feel him paying attention to me with every inch of his being. He wanted to know me. My skin tightened with the pleasure of it. So I answered.

I started talking about Cleveland, the gray streets, the olive-colored water of Lake Erie, the flat greenish Cuyahoga River, no ocean anywhere. I told him about how Tick and I were always together when we were kids, how we would fight but then, always, Tick would come back to me, sticking his head shyly around the corner of the door of my room, grinning. I said, "Tick always seemed to be wanting something. I could make him laugh, but I couldn't make him settle down. And then he started drinking. At first it was experimenting. The way kids do. The way you don't worry about too much. And then it wasn't. And we didn't know what to do. We didn't even talk about it for a long time. It was just like with my father. He was drunk most of my childhood. Just sat in the living room like a rock."

"Does he still drink?" he asked.

"No. He's been sober for a pretty long time now. But it's still hard for me to talk to him. It's hard for me to believe it, after all this time, you know?" I went on, staring at my pant legs. I couldn't look directly at Ben—what would he see in my face if I did? "When I had to go back to Cleveland a few months ago, right in the middle of a study, and leave my work and leave Daniel and get Tick out of rehab, I pretended that it was only what I was supposed to do, that I didn't mind. But I hated him. I hated being back there. I hate it."

The skin on my face felt tight. I'd never said this out loud to anyone. What was I doing? Ben was just looking at me.

"So you don't want to be the one to save him."

"I don't. I can't." I closed my eyes. "I can't." Here's what I didn't say: That it was my job to protect my brother. To save him. And I had failed.

"Of course you can't." His voice was almost a whisper. "How could you?" He stood up. "We have a little while before we have to get back. Come walk with me?" I stood up. I would do whatever he asked.

We went down the hill to the beach and took our shoes off. It was a bright March day, but a little cold to be out, so we were there alone. We walked a while, not speaking. "You're really beautiful, you know," he said after a long while. "It was the first thing I noticed about you. How beautiful you are and how you didn't seem to know it."

I had been waiting for him to say something else about Tick. I was so surprised that I laughed out loud. I pulled him to me without another thought, our brief contemplation of not doing this thing forgotten. I kissed him right out there in the sun, with nothing between us, nothing holding us apart. It was only a matter of time now. He was where I belonged.

WHEN HE ASKED ME to go on a long bike ride with him the following weekend, I did it without hesitation. I can't even remember what I told Daniel. I just had one thing I had to do and that was be with Ben. I was in kind of a trance.

The day of our ride was a perfect day. I mean really perfect. You know when the air is a tonic, and the sun is gentle and loving on your head and your shoulders, and the breeze blows like it was designed for your skin and your skin alone? It was one of those days.

We had decided that we really wanted to go some distance, so we met in Barnstable, about twenty miles from Woods Hole. There's a beautiful beach there that leads to a network of bike paths along the ocean. Part of it goes right past our part of the Woods Hole campus—there's a little office cabin facing the water there. The cabin is full of old phone books and misplaced files and other detritus—it's hardly ever used anymore. We all had keys to it—sometimes I would walk down there when I wanted some solitude and a view of the ocean.

Ben and I met, locked up our respective cars, and got going without much talk. He went ahead of me. I didn't feel the need to say anything. I just looked at him. We stopped once to drink some water and rest. I think we talked about what a beautiful day it was—nothing special.

When we got near the office cabin, I yelled, "Hey, Ben, let's stop here." He pulled over. "Are you okay?"

"I'm fine. I have a key to that office. Want to go in there for a minute?" I knew what I was saying. So did he. So we rolled our bikes up to the side of the cabin that wasn't visible from the road. He stood so closely behind me that I could feel his breath on my neck. It made me dizzy.

Once we were inside, we stood still for a minute trying to act as though nothing was happening. Then he slid his arms around my waist. There was a lot of quiet breathing and the sound of the ocean outside. Words had been removed from my mind. The silence got larger. I felt like I might die inside it, that we might stand there, him embracing me, until the end of the world and I would never say another word. I was thinking that until he said, Oh, Christ, Josie, come on. His voice was hoarse and soft. I turned to face him. He put his hand under my chin gently. Let me look at you, he said. Let me look at you. I didn't turn away or close my eyes. He kept gazing at me, so long that I thought that might be all he wanted. But then he pulled my head toward him and we started kissing. After a while, he said it again. Let me look at you. I knew what he meant. I stood up and took a few steps away from him. I took off my shorts and then my shirt with a lot of awkward wriggles and twists like I was in my bedroom at home and I wasn't embarrassed and he said, My God. You are so beautiful. He paused. And then he reached out and pulled me toward him and we started kissing again, kissing everywhere. He tasted of salt. He smelled of the sun. I thought it might never end.

Fifteen

Josie and I have been married for nearly four years. I married her to see if I could get behind that sharp unforgiving gaze. Sometimes, I think about the way she looked the day I met her, giving her oh-so-intelligent talk about undersea mammals. The way she stood with her feet planted a little bit apart, like she was going to be challenged any minute (later that very day, I saw that she *was* challenged every minute, that there are people in our business who didn't think she had any right to be there).

She's beautiful. She doesn't think so. She's not conventionally pretty and she wears her hair super-short and doesn't fuss with herself much. But her skin is so warm-colored and inviting that it always makes me feel like racism is actually based in jealousy that black people are so much better looking. And her smile, rarely bestowed, makes you feel like you've won a prize.

I try to hang on to those feelings—but it's hard these days. Ever since she picked her brother up from rehab, she's been skittish, either avoiding me or snapping at me. She's always that way after a visit home. Home has never been where her heart is. She won't even talk to me about it much. I've met everyone, of course, and I know that her father and brother both have (or in the case of her father, had) big problems with alcohol. But shared anecdotes? This-happened-to-me-when-I-was-kid stories? None of that. It's like she sprang full-blown from the sea. That's what she'd like me to think anyway.

She seems, sometimes, to have genuinely forgotten large portions of her childhood. I'll ask her about something or tell her some story about when I was a kid and a slightly blank, slightly nervous look will come over her face and she'll say, "Yeah. I don't know. It's weird. I don't remember stuff like that." I used to worry that she was one of those women with all those repressed memories of being molested, that some horrifying thing would come roaring up from her subconscious and engulf us both. I've never told her that though. I can just imagine the look that she'd give me if I did. The steel doors that would slam shut in her eyes.

She has those same walls of terror with her family. It's

not too bad with her mother but watching her talk to her father (which she does only rarely) is to watch her shrink into an agonizingly shy, angry thirteen-year-old. It's the only time I've ever seen her bite her nails. And though she keeps a picture of her and her brother, Tick, as children on her bureau, she hardly ever talks to him either. One time, kind of out of the blue when we were sitting together in the living room right after one of those calls, I asked her about it.

"You are so nervous when you talk to your family—or you don't want to talk to them at all. It's really something, Jose."

She looked at me, warily. "What do you mean?"

"I mean that your voice gets squeaky and you can't sit still and you look like you're about to jump out of your skin. What did they do?"

She bit her lip and looked away from me. "You don't understand, Danny. They . . . my brother and my father, with the booze. You know. They just . . ." She was silent a long minute. When she spoke, she looked steadily at the sofa cushion. "I'm afraid they'll take me down with them. I just can't let them in."

I took her in my arms. My heart sustained a small crack for her that night. But as I sat there with my arms around her, her face pressed into my chest, I felt her tightening against me. I felt that unyielding growing back over her skin, over her heart, over her soul. I thought that loving her would wear that unyielding down. That's what I hoped anyway.

A FEW WEEKS AGO, she went out on a dive to examine some of the institute's equipment and check on some whales they'd been tracking. She called me after to see if I wanted to meet her and the other divers for a drink, but I turned her down. I was in the middle of finishing a big grant proposal and I didn't want to stop. She got home that night after I was asleep.

The next morning, she climbed on top of me before the alarm even went off, before the sun was up. She was everywhere, kissing and sucking and whispering. I was surprised—she's not usually like this—but I sure as hell wasn't gonna stop her. Afterward, she lay with her head on my chest. "Good morning," I said. She laughed, "Good morning."

"That was a great way to wake up. What got you all worked up?"

I could only see the top of her head. "I just felt like it. You know, just turned on. I get like that after a dive."

She does, but she hadn't been like that for a while, ever since we got into this whole baby thing. I pulled her a little closer and didn't say any more.

THE STORY EVERYBODY KNOWS about infertility these days is about a woman's desperation. How the couple, usually driven by the wife, will do anything, anything to get that baby. Hock the house, sell the family jewels, have sex standing on her head in the middle of the street if necessary. Anything. But that's not Josie.

We'd been trying for about three months, and she'd just gotten her period again. She didn't tell me but I saw a tampon wrapped up in the trash. We were at breakfast when I brought it up.

"Jose, why didn't you tell me you got your period?"

"I have to tell you when I get my period now?" she said incredulously.

"You know we don't have a lot of time to waste. We shouldn't try for too long without seeing a doctor if nothing happens."

A door closed in her face right after I said that. "Is that what you want?"

"No, but if we want to have a baby, we might have to." Somehow, we had never talked this through.

"I don't know, Danny. I don't think I want to go through all that. I mean, if it happens, great, but if not. . . ."

"Look, Jose, you know as well as I do that our chances are slipping every day. Don't you even want to try?"

"We *are* trying."

"You know what I mean. Do everything we can."

She drew in a deep breath and looked deep into her cup of coffee. "No, Danny, to tell the truth, I don't."

What? What was I supposed to do now? She was the one with the uterus. If she didn't want to go further, we wouldn't. I didn't say anything more that morning or that evening, or in any of the mornings or evenings since that day, about a month ago. But we started touching each other less and less after that, the absence of her swelling belly creating a space between us. We hadn't had sex in about two or three weeks so when she climbed on me all revved up like that, it felt good. Hell, it felt great. But it didn't fix anything. It didn't get her pregnant. It didn't make me feel like she loved me.

Sixteen

A Sunday afternoon. Ben and I are together at his house, in bed. Since Leslie left, we are free to meet there, and because he doesn't live anywhere near me, I can manage it. I'm grateful Daniel and I have two cars, even though I sometimes feel guilty about how much gas we use. I almost never feel guilty about Ben. He has become as necessary to me as air. Or so it seems.

He smells like the ocean, salty and fresh and unexpected. I love that about him. That and how warm his skin always is. He told me once that his normal temperature is a couple of degrees higher than 98.6; some people's are, you know. I am licking various parts, his hipbones, his shoulders, kind of moving around, grazing his chest with mine the way I know he likes. He is kissing the parts I have guided him to over and over. We have figured how to please each other over and over. I try to keep my eyes open the whole time I'm making love with him, even when I'm coming. I don't want to miss any of it.

But the last few weeks, I've felt a slow, steady sliding away. I don't even know how I know it. It has made me wild and a little desperate when I'm with him. I keep whispering in his ear, "I'll do whatever you want." And he moves me around and kisses me and touches me but I don't feel my wildness being met by his anymore. It was at first. But now he can get enough of me.

Afterward, we lie together. Sometimes I wish we could go out more. I wonder if that would make a difference, being able to be out together like a couple. Anyway, his hand is on my stomach and we are both breathing heavily. I roll over toward him and look directly into his eyes. They are so utterly, richly brown. Like mine. "Ben, do you want to be with me?"

He laughs a little. "I think I'm with you right now."

"No, I mean . . . you know . . . *be* with me. Do you want me to leave Daniel? You never ask me to." I pause. "I would if you asked me to."

His hand goes still on my hip. "You would?"

I feel as though I can no longer breathe normally. Part

of my brain is asking why I'm even going down this road. Do I even mean what I'm saying? I'm not sure I would leave Daniel for Ben. But I can't stand watching him slip away. "I would."

Ben doesn't say anything. Then he takes his hand off of my hip and rolls onto his back. "That's an awfully big decision, Josie."

I sit up. We are not touching each other anymore. Rage is forming a rocket in my chest. "Yeah, but I would make it. I would make it for you."

"I don't know if I can ask you that, Josie. I just don't know how I'd feel about it, if you did that. If . . ."

"If what? I'm thirty-six years old. I can decide things for myself. If we want to be together badly enough, we can be. If you want it. If *we* want it."

He swings his legs over the side of the bed. He gets up, picks up his shorts and underwear, and sits back down to pull them on, his back to me. Then he speaks. "Well, I don't know if I want it."

The air goes still. "What do you mean?"

He's getting up now. I want to pull him back in bed with me. "I mean that I don't know if I want to go on with you . . . in some kind of permanent way. What we're doing. . . . Well, Jesus, Josie, sometimes I don't *know* what we're doing." His back is to me, he's sitting on the edge of the bed. He doesn't turn around. "I still want to be with you. But I don't know how I'd feel if you gave up everything for me."

"But I'd be getting what I want. It'd be worth it to me to give up something to get something. To get you. To get to be with you." My voice is high in my ears. It breaks. I hate the sound of it.

He doesn't turn around. "I'm not sure it's what I want. Or that I want to get it that way."

My chest caves in at this. Can't he hear it? He must be able to hear it crash, my breastbone breaking open, blood all over the sheets. I struggle to keep my voice level. "Well, what *do* you want?"

"I don't know. I don't know, Josie." His back is still to me. His skin is so seamless over the muscles and bone. "I really don't know. But I'm not sure it's this."

Before I know I'm even going to do it, I've hit him between the shoulder blades as hard as I can. I've turned into a crazy lady. He wheels around and looks at me, shocked. "Josie?"

"What the fuck is this then? What have we been doing?" I'm so loud. I'm so loud and crazy.

"You need to go now. We can talk about this when you've calmed down." He's standing over me now, clenching and unclenching his hands. I know he'd like to hit me. I can't seem to stop shouting. "I mean it, Ben, what the fuck is this? If you're not gonna be with me and we're just gonna go on like this. Well, what the fuck?"

"Josie, you're not making sense. We never talked about trying to make this permanent."

He is fully dressed now and I'm still naked, which makes me feel even crazier. I pull the sheet up over my breasts. He was just touching them. He was just kissing them ten minutes ago. How could this be happening? What is happening? He sits back down on the side of the bed, slightly calmed. He won't hit me now. I'm crying, not angry anymore. My chest is very tight. It's hard to breathe. "Josie. I didn't want to come to this this way. But I don't know what's gonna happen here. I'm not sure I can give you what you want. I'm not sure I can be what you need. I don't know if I'm the one."

"I do. I think we're supposed to be together. I do."

"That's not enough, just thinking that. Just *you* thinking that."

"Ben, I . . ."

"Here." He holds out my shirt to me. "You'd better get dressed. We can't talk about this anymore right now. You ought to go home."

I just look at him. He doesn't touch me. Then I put my shirt on like a chastised child. I walk into the bathroom and splash water on my face. When I would get to crying too hard in college over whatever a college girl might cry hard over, my roommate Sandra always took me firmly by the hand and marched me down the hall to splash cold water on my face. She wasn't particularly loving or gentle as she did that. But somehow her very firmness made me feel loved. I don't feel loved now.

I come out of the bathroom and stand in the doorway. Ben is standing with his back to me, looking out his bedroom window. His shoulders look strong, like they always do. He has a thin, efficient body—he was probably very gangly as a boy. Sometimes I wish I could see pictures of him when he was a teenager, squinting through his glasses. "Ben?" My voice is very small. He turns to face me. "I'm gonna go now. I love you."

"I know you do," he says. "Be careful going home, okay?"

I find my way to the door, blind, and step out onto the porch, blind, and make my way to my car, blind. How can I find anything now? How can I find anything now?

I MADE MY WAY out to the car, got in, drove. I couldn't go right home, not in the state I was in. I drove around, back and forth, up and down, trying to calm down. I wished I'd told a girlfriend about Ben so I'd have someone to call and weep to on my cell phone. But this is such a small, small town—I didn't feel like I could say anything to anyone. So I drove. After a while, I found myself thinking not about Ben but about my father. I'm not sure why, but there it was.

He got sober a few months after he moved out, near the end of my senior year of high school, after I knew I'd be going to Stanford. After he was sober and had been gone from the house for a while, I began to visit him, cautiously. Tick was busy running the streets so we never went together and, at first, I was very nervous. We'd sit in the kitchen and talk awkwardly about this and that. Daddy was quiet, contemplative. He'd begun reading again. "I read *Invisible Man* again over the last few months," he said to me on one visit. "It was good to go back to where I started from. I know you're not much of a one for novels, Josie, but you liked that one, right?" I nodded. There was a lot of it that I didn't understand but a lot I loved, nevertheless.

I was always uncomfortable during these visits. I couldn't forget the looming silences, the nasty remarks, the beer stench I grew up with. What happened to that man? How'd I know he wasn't going to reappear?

And then of course, he did. It was just before I left for my senior year of college. I took the bus over to his house—my mother needed the car for something—and rang his bell. He came to the door in his undershirt, which was my first clue; he didn't do that kind of thing anymore. He was always nicely dressed. "Hey, baby girl," he said.

"Daddy? Are you all right?"

He rubbed his face. "Yeah, yeah, I'm fine. Whyn't you come on in, I'll get us something to eat." He leaned forward to kiss me and I smelled it on him. I lost it—kind of like I did with Ben. I have never been so angry in my life, I didn't know what I was going to do until I did it. I shoved him away from me, shouting as I did it. "You're drunk, aren't you? Admit it! Admit it! Goddamn it, admit it, you've been drunk almost my whole goddamn life." I *pushed* him; I pushed my big father back into the doorway of his apartment. I pushed him away from me. I kept yelling, "Why should I believe anything you say to me? You spent your whole life like this disgusting, miserable mess. I'm not dealing with it anymore. I'm done!" I ran out, crying. I could hear his voice behind me but I didn't stop. I didn't dare stop. I cried the whole way home on the bus as people strenuously avoided looking at me. Once I got off the bus, I stood on the corner long enough for my face to dry. I took a lot of deep breaths. And when I got home, I didn't tell my mother anything. But I'll tell you something that I knew in that moment. I was done with him. He wasn't getting another chance.

I've stuck with that. He apologized to me about the whole thing a few months afterward; that slip didn't become a binge. The apology was part of his making amends, I guess. After he made his little speech, we hugged each other. But I didn't believe him. Not really. I didn't dare. I couldn't stand the disappointment when he failed me again.

There is a great deal of evidence that shows that addiction lies in the brain, in its very makeup. That's why not everyone can quit; sometimes you just can't outrun that circuitry. It seemed my father had done it—he had certainly been sober for a long time since that slip. I was furious but not too blind to see that. But even so, if it was in your brain, it was in your brain. I understood that now, in my bones. Because that's how I was with Ben. After that fight with Ben, after I got myself together, I told myself sternly that I had to pull away a little, but then I would take one look at him and it was like being hit with a two-by-four. I was felled by desire. I wanted to feel the way I felt—the way we felt—that first time we made love. That's an addiction, of course. But you can never get back that first high. You just keep looking for it, no matter how much damage you cause.

Seventeen

Tick woke up . . . where? He didn't know where. There was a leg thrown across his, a heavy, smooth, brown one. He supposed he ought to take some pleasure in this. It seemed to be a woman's leg. But he couldn't remember anything about the person it was attached to, where he was, how he'd gotten there. The room smelled of cigarette smoke. He coughed and his head pounded, slowly, rhythmically. His tongue felt like sandpaper and his nose was running. The owner of the leg snored and rolled away. A name distantly floated into his head. Tonya? Was that it? He lay there. Looking at the ceiling. Yellow, pockmarked with cracks. He'd begun his evening in a bar. He did remember that.

He was supposed to stay out of bars now. They were bad for him. Full of what ailed him. Packed with nothing but his sorrow, Mom's and Daddy's broken hearts, my disdain, everything he wanted to avoid. But last night, without warning, that siren song struck up again Just like that.

The funny thing about his slip was, just like they said in all those twelve-step meetings, it wasn't a special day or a special occasion or like he'd decided *Damn it, I'm gonna drink again.* He didn't even know it was starting when it started. There was this girl, one of the many girls who were always around the parking lot at the end of the day hoping for the slightest magic touch from one of the magic men on the team. Or even someone associated with the team. Someone like him. This girl was a little more desperate, a little more used up. The players, all of them so young and strong and full of themselves, could smell it on her. None of them took her, the casual way they'd take one girl and not the other; sometimes they'd take two. But they didn't even see her. When Tick came out of the locker room into the late-afternoon sun and headed toward his not-giant, not-shiny car, she sashayed up to him with a big open smile, and said, "Well, what do you do for the team?"

"I'm a trainer."

She took a step toward him. "Ooh, a trainer. Does that

mean you get to go to practices and work with the players?" She took another step. "Did you used to work with LeBron?"

In fact, he never had. Only the most trusted senior trainers got anywhere near that priceless body. But she was looking at him with such steady admiration. It had been so long since a woman had looked at him like that. What would be the harm? "I used to. It was kind of fucked up the way he left with that ESPN shit. But he had to do what was right for him. I get it."

She shifted her body in a way that let him know she was his for the evening. Just like that. "Yeah. You gotta do what's right for you." She twirled a strand of her long weave around her finger. She had long fucshia-colored fingernails. "I'd love to hear more about your job. My name's Tonya."

"Well, why don't we go get a drink and I can tell you all about it."

When he said that, he was thinking he'd just stick to Coke. No harm in that. No harm in sitting with a girl and having a Coke, right? It was like something out of one of those fifties shows like *Leave It to Beaver.* So they got in his car and they drove and they found a little place called Pedro's.

It was a golden-colored late afternoon. The downtown streets had that internal quietude that so much of Cleveland seemed to have. Tonya chattered away—something about the Cavs—but he wasn't really listening. For some reason, he thought of me, how much I hated Cleveland. He didn't understand why I felt the way I did. He was used to his city. Its small grayness felt like home to him.

They entered the bar. There was the neon, the friendly neon he always loved. This time it touted the virtues of Heineken. There was the gentle wood glow of the bar. There was a small patch of afternoon sunlight on the floor in the back. It looked inviting. They sat in the back, not at the bar. It was safer there. The leather was warm and giving, like skin, like the skin of someone he loved. Tonya was still talking. When was the last time he had touched a woman he loved? When was the last time he'd touched a woman's skin at all? When he wasn't watching TV, he spent a lot of time jacking off like a lonely teenage boy. He leaned back against the seat. A tired-looking waitress, the only one in the place, asked them what they wanted. He ordered a burger and a Coke. Tonya ordered a cosmopolitan. What they brought her looked something like Kool-Aid in a martini glass. The hamburger was surprisingly good, a little charred on the outside and rare on the inside, not overhandled, just the way he liked them. The Coke was fine. It was a Coke. When the waitress came back to ask them if they wanted anything else, he asked for a Corona. He didn't think of the steps. He didn't think of calling anyone. He thought it would be okay. She went to get it. She didn't make anything special of his request. He drank it as soon as she brought it. Not frantically. But with a quiet, sober pleasure. Then he ordered another one. He put his hand onto Tonya's thigh and she quit talking and smiled, looking down at the table as though she'd been told a secret. That was pretty much it for the sobriety. The next thing he remembered was that cold, cold morning and that leg thrown over him in an apartment he didn't recognize. He sat up. He wished he had a beer right then. Was that all there is to it? Just giving in? He wondered if he could get out of the apartment before Tonya woke up. God only knew what they'd done together. God only knew. That's the only one who could help him now, he feared. God Almighty. And despite what he'd said over and over in all those AA meetings, he wasn't at all sure about that guy's existence.

Eighteen

So after he left Tonya's house was the beginning. It didn't take long to get to the middle—a couple of weeks, maybe? He wasn't sure where the end would be. But he wasn't there yet. This part, he remembered. There was the enormous pleasure at first. But it was gone quickly. Then there was only the need. The drink he had to have. The hit he had to buy, the rush and run of it. He got to the middle so much faster this time. He wasn't even enjoying it anymore.

It didn't take long for them to see it on him at work. So it didn't take long for Bob Trumbull to call him into his office and, with eyes that looked like he'd just seen his best friend lying dead in the street, say, "Tick, I gotta let you go. This was your last chance." Tick protested—"Just one slip. Give me another chance. I'm not going back there, no sir"—and Bob looked at him with a gaze so gentle and unconvinced that Tick was afraid he might cry and rather than do that he stood up and left the office and went to his locker and got his stuff and left the arena and that was that. That was the end of one thing he loved.

When he told Mom about losing the job, her mouth tightened and her eyes hollowed out. But she said nothing. She didn't ask him to leave and she didn't ask any questions, which surprised him.

Within a month, he almost wished she had put him out. Or screamed at him, or something. He wanted someone to react. He was drinking every day. Plus he had been thinking about the sweet sharp sting of coke up his nose for two days straight, and so he had decided to try that again. He'd never used it much, but he wanted it now. He hadn't been to an AA meeting since he lost his job. He carried the pocket-sized meeting schedule with him and, sometimes, he'd run his finger over the edge, but there was something that wouldn't let him go. Instead, he found himself rifling through his mother's top drawer, looking for money.

After he took the seventy-five dollars that he found and jammed it into his pocket, he went out to find a pay phone to call his old dealer. He'd take his mother's money but he still had a scruple or two left. He didn't want to call his dealer from her phone. He wished he still had a cell. It was so damn hard to find a pay phone these days.

After a lot of driving around, he found a greasy pay phone at a decrepit convenience store. It had taken forever and it looked like it was going to rain and the wind had an edge. He was surprised at how easily Beenie's number came back to him, though. Like he'd never been away. Clearly kept in his head where the important stuff was. Beenie's voice, always slow and half asleep, answered.

"Yo."

"Yo, Beenie, it's Tick."

"Tick? Tick? Man, I thought you was walking the straight and narrow."

"Yeah, well, it got a little too narrow, you know." A song blasted tinnily from the little transistor behind the counter. The counterman—dark-eyed and dark-skinned but not black, Pakistani or something—eyed Tick suspiciously. Tick turned away and lowered his voice, like the criminal he had become. "Listen, are you holding?"

"Now, come on, man, when I ever do you wrong? I'm always holding. I got what you need, my brother." He paused. "So you're back, huh?"

"Yeah." Tick took a deep breath and stared at the graffiti-covered wall behind to the phone. "I'm back."

• • •

TWENTY MINUTES LATER, he was standing on Beenie's porch, dripping wet from the downpour that had just begun. Actually, it was Beenie's aunt's house, about two blocks from where we grew up. Not far from where Tick used to ride bikes when he was a kid, before Dean, before all this, with his friends Kenny and Dwayne and Alan. All of them had gone off to do something with themselves after a few years of fooling around, acting like nothing wasn't ever gonna change, nothing wasn't ever gonna be good enough. And then they found good enough. Found good jobs and good women. Well, all but that knucklehead Dwayne—he was locked up in Mansfield for fifteen years. Armed robbery. And Tick. For a while, he thought he'd be like Kenny and Alan, that he'd be able to put the foolishness down someday. He'd even done it. He'd done it! Twice! But then he picked it up again, after a few clean months. He was gonna have to ride this train to the end. Because he couldn't put it down.

Beenie seemed happy to see him. As happy as he ever was to see anybody. He had on a black do-rag and a white tank top. He'd clearly been spending time at the gym—Beenie didn't use. He only sold. He knew which side his bread was buttered on. He was rubbing his face as he opened the door. "So, my man Tick. Welcome back. What can I do for you?"

What could Beenie do for him? Refuse to sell him anything and send him home, he thought bitterly, that's the best thing Beenie could do for him. But he said, "I need to get straight and I ain't got that much money. What can you do for me with seventy-five dollars?"

Beenie told him. It wasn't much. But it was something. The deal was made, the money exchanged, the package in his hand. But he had nowhere to go with it—Mom's basement? No. No. Not there. He stood irresolute for a few minutes. Beenie's aunt kept her eyes and her mind closed to what was going on in her house. So Beenie had not only his own bedroom but a small off-to-the-side room for those who needed to cop immediately and had nowhere else to go. Tick had always thought that room was for the lowest of the low. He never thought he'd have to go to that room. Except now he did. He looked at Beenie for a minute. Beenie took a long drag on his cigarette and looked at Tick indifferently. "You need to go on back there, man? Get right? Well, go on. You know the deal. It's a girl back there but it's no one you know."

Tick nodded, wordlessly. Beenie's aunt kept three or four cats that had the run of the place. The house smelled of old sweat and cat piss. He went to the back room, where the door was half open; he pushed on it lightly and entered.

There was a sofa that was all cotton-sprung and sagging, covered with what had once been brown corduroy, but now? Hard to say. It was moldering with sweat and spilled stuff. There were a couple of broken-down, equally disgusting old easy chairs and a coffee table with a mirror for doing lines or setting up whatever you needed to set up whatever way you needed to set it up. There was a girl with her skirt pushed up and her legs thrown so wide open that he could see her black lace underwear. She was white, with brittle blond ends and long dark roots. She was maybe twenty-five. She had dark, dark circles under her eyes. Her head lolled back on the sofa and her works sat on the table. She was already long, long gone to wherever the heroin took her. It occurred to Tick—he didn't know why, he didn't really want to do it—that he probably could have climbed right on top of her there and had her and she never even would have known it. Her breathing seemed to fill the room.

Well. He had somewhere he needed to get to. Better get going. He poured out a little of the coke, cut it easily and expertly, and snorted it. It was, as they say, like riding a bike—one of those things you never truly forget how to do.

He kept going until he was so high that he couldn't keep still and so horny he couldn't think. Coke always got to him like that. He moved next to the girl and slid his hand up her exposed thigh. She stirred slightly but didn't come out of her nod and didn't move away. He unzipped his pants and reached in. He was too high even to feel horrified by what he was doing. He was very hard. It just took a few strokes of his hand to bring him off. He wiped himself off with the girl's discarded sweatshirt. He felt relieved at first but then, for a second, everything became clear. He was so disgusted with himself that he had to do another line, so he could forget who he'd turned into. So he could forget all those meetings at Riverrun, the hope he'd had when he first came home. He finished the coke. Then he left the house and went to a bar. He wasn't going to stop until he had reached the end.

THE NEXT TIME HE was aware of anything at all, he was sprawled across his bed in the basement. He was still fully dressed, and he smelled of alcohol. Mom stood over him, her face a stone. He'd never seen her look like that before. "So you're awake," she said.

"Yeah."

"That's good, because you need to pack and get out of here."

"What?" Even as he said it, he couldn't really rouse any anger. This was the price of the ticket.

"I said, you've got to go. I can't. I won't watch you kill yourself in my house. I watched your father go down for too long. I watched you go down before. I'm not going to watch it again."

Tick was silent for a moment. "Daddy stopped," he said.

"Yes, he did." She closed her eyes and finished speaking.

"Yes, he did. But only after I drew the line. I should have drawn it with you a long time ago." Her voice wavered for the first time. "You have to go," she finished.

Tick looked at her. She was immovable. "Are you just gonna stand there, Mom?"

"Until I see your bags packed and you out the door. I'll give you a little bit of money. Even though I know you've been stealing from me. Even though you'll probably just spend it on booze. But this will be the last you get from me." She reached into her pocket. Her hands shook.

When he first woke up, Tick thought he felt as bad as it was possible to feel. But he felt even worse as he took the money from our mother. She watched him pack. She stood at the door as he left. She didn't speak again, even when he said, "Bye, Mom." She nodded slightly. He looked down. Her hands were still shaking.

He wasn't sure where he would go. But he was going. He left the house, stepped out into the cool darkness, his eyes burning. His car was there but he didn't trust himself to drive. So he left his last earthly possession in the driveway. It was the least he could do. He'd take the bus. He'd take the bus to wherever he was going. He could hardly walk, he had the shakes so bad. But he wanted not to cop, not to get a drink. Not this time. He thought about how Daddy had quit after he left us. He got himself to the Greyhound station on East Ninth Street. It was a very long walk from the house, but he had to save that money. He had to keep setting down his suitcase and sitting on it. Once he had to throw up. But he made it. He went to the window. He didn't know what he was going to say until he got there. But once he was there, he asked the man how much a ticket to Woods Hole, Massachusetts, was. And he bought a ticket to come to me. He hoped he could count on me one more time.

Part Three

Nineteen

If I'd been kind enough or present enough to have listened to my father or asked him any questions during our rare, uncomfortable telephone conversations, I'd have known that, one day at a time, he truly had turned things around. He was sober and calm and even almost—dare he even think it?—happy. Well, maybe not happy. But at peace. Now that he was near seventy, he'd found that peace they talked about so much in the rooms. He hoped Tick could find it, too, but he knew it was something Tick had to do himself. Tick didn't talk to him much more than I did. He mourned the way he'd lost us, but he knew that he wasn't in control of our coming back. Maybe we would, maybe we wouldn't. It was his job to be there and be sober either way. That's what he knew now. So he made his own life as good as it could be. He'd been volunteering at the Hough branch of the public library for five years. He'd been retired for eight and he spent the first three years of his retirement reading and taking walks and seeing Natalie, a woman from the AA meeting he went to. He liked having his days completely free, but after a while, that got a little dull. That's when he started volunteering.

They say you're not supposed to date within the meetings. But he and Natalie had both been sober for a long time and they'd heard that AA slogan Take What You Like and Leave the Rest enough times that they decided they could take each other and leave the no-dating rule behind. After he committed to being sober one day at a time, he found that having someone to be with could help him keep that promise. Natalie was white. (Him with a white woman—who'da thunk it?) She was very smart and used to be a schoolteacher. They both loved to read. He especially treasured the evenings they sat together at opposite ends of the sofa, each with a book on their laps and their legs entangled, because he remembered how he had started to lose the ability to read thoughtfully at the end of his drinking days. Being able to do it again was a great gift. Natalie gave him a lot of pleasure and they had a lot of fun together, but he still missed my mother. He still thought about her laugh sometimes or the curve of her hip. When he hung up the phone after one of their brief, difficult conversations about Tick, he always wanted to pick it up again and ask her to take him back. How he hated to part from her, even on the phone, even when she didn't love him anymore. What did it matter? He would always love her.

The other thing that disturbed his peace—didn't take it away but disturbed it—was the life of the city itself. It seemed as though everything was falling apart in slow motion. Take a look at St. Clair Avenue. It used to be a vibrant main drag, full of Slovenian shops and small factories and then later a mix of little stores and restaurants and whatnot, some black-owned, some white-owned. But busy and alive. Now? Drive five blocks, see one open business. Or for another example, take the kids who hung out at the library. They didn't read—they just seemed to see the library as a place out of the weather to hang out. They had no respect, no decorum, no sense of how to act about anything. All of them black, which broke his heart. They rolled in every afternoon, every other word out of their mouth "nigger" this and "nigger" that. They didn't seem to care about anything except whatever impulse they were having at the moment they had it. It was often a destructive or disruptive one. His job at the library was to staff the desks when the librarians were on break, as the budget had been cut so severely that the library couldn't hire a lot of professional librarians. So he filled in. He answered questions and watched the scene. He had to call security about once a week about some bunch of kids or another. They made everything hard for the people who were trying to use the library properly, the little girls sitting and reading, their noses almost touching their books, the dreadlocked mothers trying to teach their kids the right way to act. He tried to talk to some of the young men sometimes, reason with them. But even if they quieted down, looked at the floor for a moment when he spoke to them, once they got back together and a little bit away from him, the noise and the raucousness and the rudeness would begin again.

So that was one sign of things falling apart. The other became clear to him when he went downtown on a weekday, something he didn't do often. He wanted to check something out from the main branch of the library, which was on Euclid, imposing and gray and beautiful like so many libraries built in the nineteenth century (I used to spend hours browsing the science shelves there). But now? The library echoed with quiet emptiness—in fact, the whole center of the city was empty. Not really—there were people there. But the push and throb that one associates with a healthy metropolis? Not there. The crowds—well, groups of people really—who had to work down there or who chose to come there to shop all looked a little dispirited and confused. For lunch, he went into a food court across the street from the library and he was the only person in there. The yellowing lettuce in the salad bar was lonely, the sandwiches looked bereft, the cashier slumped at her station, bored. At noon on a Tuesday, when everyone in an office ought to be hungry, ought to be running out with their coworkers to get something to eat, and the cashier ought to feel annoyed because she was just too busy—nothing.

He talked to Natalie about it at dinner that night. "Man, when I was downtown today at the library, it was dead. Totally dead. I tell you."

"What do you mean?"

"I mean it wasn't like a city at all. Sure wasn't the city I moved into years ago. Go into a store and the clerk's just standing there with nothing to do, all these empty storefronts and office buildings. It was sad."

"This is news to you?" Natalie said, setting down her fork with a slight snap. "Cleveland's been in rough shape for a while."

Ray sighed. "I know. But I've been living here nearly forty years now. I don't know. I remember what it used to be like."

Natalie came around the table and slid her arms around

his neck. "Well, a lot of things aren't how they used to be. But that doesn't mean how they are now is so bad, does it?"

He turned to kiss her, this kind woman who cared for him. It felt good to kiss her. He knew that there was something real there. But he felt a little heartbroken all the same. Everything he had once truly loved was slipping away from him—his city, his home, his wife, his children. No matter how much they talked in meetings about how you had to let go, how you couldn't control the circumstances of your life, every now and then he still hoped that just staying away from that bottle would fix everything. That staying sober would be enough.

The next morning, after Natalie left and he was sitting alone at his kitchen table, wondering what he would make of the day, he decided to do something he hadn't done in about three months. He decided to call me.

I never called him. But he made himself pick up the phone every few months and go through a chilly, awkward conversation with me. His heart hurt after every call, but he did it anyway—reaching out was part of his amends. He always went to a meeting after we talked. It was either that or have a drink.

So he took a deep breath and picked up the phone. I answered on the third ring.

"Hey, Josie-girl. It's Dad."

"Hi, Daddy."

"I've been wondering how you're doing."

"I'm all right. Busy working. You know." I kept typing as I spoke, the phone tucked uncomfortably between shoulder and ear. What could he know of my life? I didn't want to tell him anything, especially now.

"What are you working on?"

"I'm working on a paper about the effect of LFA sonar on sperm whales. I have to present it in a couple of weeks." Click. Click.

"Oh, yeah? What's LFA sonar?"

"Low frequency active sonar. The navy uses it to track submarines, but it makes such a loud sound in the ocean that the whales freak out and surface too fast, and it gives them the bends, like divers get when they surface too fast."

"Really? That's terrible."

"Yeah." Silence.

Finally my father spoke.

"So how have you been?"

"You asked that already, Daddy. I'm fine. How are you?"

"I'm good. Volunteering over in Hough still. Them little roughnecks in there about to drive me crazy sometimes."

"Yeah?"

"Well, I just wanted to see how you were doing. How's Daniel?"

"He's fine. We're both fine."

"That's good. Have you talked to Tick?"

"No. I haven't." I couldn't go down the Tick road right this minute; my head would explode if I did. So I cut him off. "Listen, Daddy, I'm kind of up against it here, so maybe we could talk later?" My voice shook a little. When I was little, I would have given anything for him to pay this kind of attention to me.

He didn't say this to me, but he knew there would be no later. "Sure, baby. Sure. Just call when you can talk."

"Okay."

"Take care of yourself."

"Okay. You, too."

"I will. That's how I make it. Taking each day as it comes."

I sighed. What was I supposed to say to that? "Okay, bye, Daddy." I left my hand on the phone after I hung up as though he could see it there, see that I didn't quite want to let go. I bit my lip. Okay. Okay. That's done now. I'm done with him now.

On his end of the phone, now silent, he too held the receiver a little longer than necessary. It was ten-thirty in the morning. He had an AA meeting at noon and then there was a movie he wanted to get to afterward. He had always loved going to the movies, and he still thrilled to the retired man's luxury of going in the middle of the day. He looked out the window, my crisp, distant voice still sounding in his ears. It felt as though it was going to be a long day.

Twenty

The day after I talked to Daddy, our phone rang around six a.m. I picked it up, confused, my heart pounding from the crush of noise that a ringing telephone makes when it wakes you from a sound sleep. "Hello? Hello?"

There was only deep sobbing on the other end of the line. I listened for a minute, confused. Then I realized that it was my mother. "Mom? What is it? What's going on?"

Finally, she spoke. "Your brother . . ." By this time Daniel had awakened and embraced me from behind, his hand on my hip, automatically.

"What about Tick, Mom?"

"He came home drunk or high or something. I don't know, sometime last night. He's started stealing from me. I put him out. I can't go through any more. I just can't. I don't even know where he is." She sobbed again. "He might come to you. I'm afraid he might come to you."

"Right," I said. I didn't know what else to say. "Right." I stopped again. "How would he get here, Mom?"

"How do I know?" she almost screamed. "I don't know anything about him anymore. How the hell do I know?" Then her voice softened abruptly. "He loves you, Josie. And he's got nowhere else to go. He might have enough for the bus—he left his car." She sighed. "I gave him some money when he was getting his things together. Even though I know he's been stealing. I didn't know if he had any left. I couldn't get myself to send him away without anything. I probably should have. But I couldn't." She started crying again.

"Okay, okay, Mom." I rubbed my forehead as hard as I could. "I guess all we can do is get some sleep now. You tried his cell phone, right?"

"He doesn't have one anymore. They cut off his service."

"Of course. Well, look, we'll just see. We'll just have to see. Don't worry. We'll keep talking, and I'll let you know as soon as anything happens up here."

"Okay." She sounded very old, older than the last time I talked to her. Older than she was when she got up that morning, probably. How little I knew her. "Okay. But I guess there's nothing else to say, is there?"

"I don't think so, Mom. I don't know what else to say."

"All right, then, baby. I'm sorry. I'm really sorry. I'm sorry you have to start your day like this. You let me know what happens."

"I will." And then she hung up.

I stayed on my side, unmoving, my hand clutching the phone so hard that it hurt. Daniel breathed behind me for a minute. "What happened, Josie? Something at home?"

His voice unmoored me from my frozen position. I hung up the phone carefully, like it would break, and rolled onto my back. I had a sudden flash of me crying in Ben's arms over exactly this something at home just a few months ago. "Yeah, Danny. Tick's gone. My mother threw him out. He's drinking again. Or using again. Or something. Mom thought he might be coming up here to us. To me." I stared at the ceiling. There was pressure behind my eyes. But I wasn't crying. I felt salty. Alone. Despite Daniel lying next to me. Despite the fact that I had a lover that I would do anything for. Despite the fact that my eyes were growing wet. I felt like the middle of the Sahara, a place I've never been. I felt as though the sun had eaten my bones. I felt like a woman with no brother, no husband, no one to call her own.

"So what do you think Tick's gonna do?" Daniel said.

"I have no idea," I said. "I can't believe he'd come here. Maybe he would. But how would he even get here? What's he doing for money? I have no idea." I turned toward him and Daniel pulled my head onto his chest and I had a sudden moment of thinking I should say everything. That I should tell him about Ben and about what it was like to have Tick for a brother and everything. That I should tell him every bit of me. But I couldn't figure out how we'd ever have that conversation. I'd held back too much for too long. So I just lay there and let him comfort me like he has so many times before. How much do we ever really know another person anyway? How much should we ever say to another person? About anything? Should I have told him how much I used to love Tick? Tick was how I measured myself in the world. He was my template. How I missed that guy. He'd been gone for many years. But I missed him every day. I didn't say this to Daniel. I couldn't find the words. So we just lay there for a while. Silent. Then Daniel put his hand on my stomach. I welcomed it. Making love seemed like the only possible response to what was going on. It would let us push everything else aside. So we made love. For our separate reasons. And then the day began.

• • •

OUTSIDE, THE SUN BLEACHED everything to blankness. I went into the shower without grabbing a robe, but Daniel didn't look at me. He stayed in bed until I was done. I was glad he didn't come in. The water felt like a kind of forgiveness. I suppose he just looked at the ceiling the whole time. That's what he was doing when I came out. He got up with a sad smile when I sat on the edge of the bed to dress. What was he thinking? I didn't want to know.

We had breakfast and had our coffee and didn't talk about Tick. I didn't know what to say. Whatever was going to be was simply going to be. As I drove to work, the roads seemed more twisty than usual. I almost missed the turnoff to the institute. I couldn't pay attention. My throat hurt. My cell phone rang just as I pulled into the parking lot and turned off the ignition. It was Ben. I had to close my eyes and rest my head on the steering wheel, shaking all over. That's how relieved I was to hear his voice.

"How are you?"

"I'm all right. I'm all right, I guess."

"You don't sound all right," he said gently, "What's going on?"

"What's going on? What's going on? I wish I knew. All I know is that my mother threw Tick out of the house and now she thinks he might be coming up here to me. It's just all too much." I was silent for a minute. "I miss you."

"I miss you, too." Then he laughed a little. "But I'll see you inside in a few minutes. How high school is this?"

I laughed a little too loudly and hung up. But I sat for a minute, holding the phone to my chest. Like it was his hand. My heart rattled inside my ribcage. I thought about Tick for a minute. And then I felt sick and had to get out of the car.

Twenty-one

It took Tick a little more than twenty-four hours to get to me on the bus. Twenty-four hours of shivering. Twenty-four hours of not eating and drinking lukewarm water from an old Poland Spring bottle as he stared miserably out the window. There were two transfers. He sat in the back of each bus, getting up periodically to vomit in the foul little bathroom that he was making fouler, then returning to huddle in his seat. At one stop a mother with three little kids got on. She was herding and fussing as they came near him to use the bathroom. When they came out, the mother took a long look at him. Then she compressed her lips into a thin line and took her little boy's hand and marched her children, firmly, back to the front of the bus. They didn't look like they had much money. But they knew a fucked-up junkie alcoholic when they saw one. And as beat down as they were, the mother guided her children away. Tick would have killed for a beer. But he couldn't get one. He looked outside at the flat, dirty landscape going by. They were driving down a depressing highway with only scrubby plants and squat buildings next to it. The skies were weeping rain. He stared out the window.

He arrived at the tiny bus station in Woods Hole at about ten on a bustling Saturday morning. He had been straight for long enough now that, though he still craved a drink, his body had calmed down a little. He felt nearly human.

He wasn't quite sure how he'd find my house. He'd never been to visit me before. He had my address, so he could ask someone how to find the street, but who knew how far away it might be? The bus shelter was right in the middle of the town's business section, so he made his way to a nearby café. The ocean, he noted, came right up to the edges of the town. He also spotted a bar near the bus station called the Captain Kidd. He turned his head away as if the sight of it alone would get him drunk. As he walked into the coffee shop, he noticed a flier offering assistance in staging drug and alcohol interventions on the bulletin board of the café. He smiled a little, bitterly, at this. Too bad Mom hadn't seen this in Cleveland. Before he went up to the counter, he looked down at himself. His pants were shiny with dirt and had random food stains. He ran his hand across his chest under his stretched-out sweater and felt how sweaty he was. He wished he had a mirror. And then again, he didn't. He wasn't going to like what he saw anyway.

Behind the counter was a floppy-haired white kid who couldn't have been much more than seventeen or eighteen. He was reading *Maxim* and chewing gum. Tick swallowed once, hard, and cleared his throat. "Can you tell me how to get to this address?" he said. His voice creaked. It had been so long since he'd used it. He didn't stand too close to the kid.

The kid looked up, long blond hair, sleepy, unfocused blue eyes. But then he did something surprising. He didn't act horrified or appalled by Tick. He seemed to apprehend the situation immediately. He gave him careful directions: "It's kind of a long walk, but you can make it. You don't have a car, right?" He offered Tick a bottle of water: "On the house, man." And told him where the bathroom was. Tick nodded—he didn't trust himself to speak again—and went to use it, to splash water on his face and under his arms. While he was in there, he did look in the mirror. His dark skin was gray, his lips grayer still and cracked. Stuff was stuck in the corners of his mouth. He breathed into his hand and was grateful he hadn't gotten closer to that nice kid—his breath would have knocked the kid over. What had happened to him? What had happened? He opened the bottle of water and drank a little. When he came out, he said, "Thank you," to the kid.

"No problem, man," the kid said, a wide, genuine smile on his face. "I think I know where you're at. I've been there myself. You stay strong, bro. Try to get to a meeting up here."

He slid a sheet of paper across the counter toward him. It was a list of local AA meetings. Tick took it. "Thanks, man."

"No problem. Take it light, all right?"

"I will. I will." He pushed his way out of the store. The air was soft against his skin.

The kid was right. It was a long walk, all uphill. He was finally beginning to feel hungry and it weakened him. But after a long while he saw our street, Daniel's and mine. He thought it was pretty. The houses were set back from the curb and each had a small front lawn and a porch. It was hard to see the addresses. Some people had those reflective numbers but many didn't. He thought he probably should have called first. But what would he have said? What on earth was there to say? He just kept walking. He was almost there.

The street was quiet and still. He checked the scrap of paper he'd written my address on again. His feet hurt and his chest was tight. He wished for a drink. But instead, he climbed the steps and rang the bell.

A year passed in silence. Then he heard footsteps. And the door opened. I can't imagine what went through his mind. Every detail of that moment is crystal in my mind. I even remember what I was wearing—a ratty old blue bathrobe that used to be Daniel's. I took one step toward Tick, then another. And then I slapped him across the face as hard as I could. Tick stood with his head turned, not touching his sore cheek, as if frozen by my touch. My heart pounded furiously and we stood there for another moment. Then he looked at me, so sad and lost, and all the anger drained out of me. How could I hit him when life was hitting him so hard already? I reached out and pulled him toward me.

"Damn it, Tick. You make me so fucking mad. I know I had no business hitting you like that but . . . damn." I said all this into his neck, holding him like a lover. His breath on my neck was hot and stale. He smelled sweaty and scared. He still hadn't said a word. Daniel came out and stood uncertainly a few feet away. With him there, I felt self-conscious and moved away from Tick. He stood there, biting his lip.

"I'm sorry, Jose. I didn't have anywhere else to go."

"I know." I sighed. "I know. Come on in." I stepped aside so he could pass.

Tick and I sat at the kitchen table and Daniel started making coffee. I could tell by the set of his back how angry he was, but he was still doing the right thing, still helping. I sat across from Tick and pulled myself together. Our hands rested on the table between us. The only sound in the room was the hiss of the coffee maker. Finally, I spoke. "Tick. Tick. What are you doing here?"

"Dag, Josie, why'd you hit me? Ain't seen me in I don't know how long and first thing you do is haul off and slap me? Damn. Ain't that about nothin'."

"I'm sorry about that, Tick. I just reacted. I've been so worried." I took another deep breath and went on. "Mom says you've been using again. I guess I hit you for her sake. I can't believe you'd do that to her again, Tick. I really can't."

Tick lowered his forehead to the table and rubbed his temple as though he was in pain. I'm sure he was. "Yeah. I can't believe it either." Daniel put a cup of black coffee in front of him without a word. He actually hadn't said a word yet—to either of us—since the doorbell rang. "Josie, you know I didn't mean to. You know I didn't mean to hurt her. That's why I came up here. I thought if I could get the hell out of Cleveland . . . you know, stay with you a while . . . that I could get clean." He lifted the coffee with shaking hands. "I thought maybe I could get clean up here. It's nice up here. I can see that already." If I could have seen his thoughts, they would have been these: The kindness of the kid in the coffee shop. The sun off the ocean downtown. Maybe a person could start again here. With the sea close at hand.

Twenty-two

And what of my good, kind Daniel during all this? When I hit Tick, he was the one who tried to make it right. When Tick needed a place to stay, he was the one who didn't say no. But he's not a saint. He's a man. He's a man I was pushing about as far as it was possible to be pushed. As the cliché has it (and as we in the sciences know), something had to give.

We sat at the table a little longer. No one seemed to know what to say. Tick stared into his black coffee as though the answer lay there. After a while he lifted his head and gave us a weak smile. "I really need something to eat and a shower and a nap," he said. Thank God. Something concrete to do.

Daniel and I both practically leapt up from the table, flying into awkward host mode, finding towels and putting sheets on the guest bed in the office and studiously not talking to each other (or even looking at each other much) until Tick was safely stowed away.

I did one other thing in this hostly flurry. While I was in our office/guest room alone making up the bed and Daniel was rooting around looking for towels, I called Ben. Right from the house—an enormous risk. I was past caring. Tick's arrival had removed the last vestige of that from me. I didn't talk to Ben for long. I just told him I needed to see him. I wished I was diving, somewhere far away from all this. Somewhere safe and cool and blue. I looked out the window. The sun splashed onto the houses across the street. My heart quieted for a moment. Then I went up to our bedroom, where Daniel sat on the edge of the bed.

"So, Jose, how about all this?"

"How about it?" I sat down beside him and sighed. "Well."

"Well what do you want to do? Have you told your mother that he's here?"

"No. No—when would I have done that?" I sounded petulant. I didn't mean to. "I'm sorry, Danny. But when would I have done that? He hasn't even been here three hours yet."

"Some people would have called their parents first thing when something like this happened. Some people would not be so afraid of where they come from."

"What?" Had he heard me on the phone with Ben?

"I just think. I've watched you run and run and run from them." He took a deep breath. "I've watched you run from me. And now he's here. Your drunk, drug-addict brother is here and you can't run anymore. Can't you try to be here with it? Be here with me?"

Something cracked in my mind. I stood up and knocked everything off my dresser, in one smooth motion. The crash made me jump, even as I thought about how dramatic the gesture was. The picture of Tick and me fell face down. I was supposed to be a rational soul. But I wasn't now. I was only impulse. Daniel jumped off the bed, shouting, "What is wrong with you, Josie? What is wrong with you?" He grabbed my wrists and I looked straight into his eyes. My breath whistled in and out, rapidly. Daniel held my wrists a little longer. We had never been in a place like this. We stared at each other. Daniel was the first to speak.

"I've been walking around like I've got a sock in my mouth for months, but I can't fucking stand it anymore.

Jesus Christ, Josie. Jesus Christ. What the fuck is going on with you?"

"Daniel, my brother just showed up with nothing left in this world. What do you think is going on with me?"

Daniel looked at me silently. Then he let go of my wrists and sat back down on the bed, like an old, old man. "Josie, it's not just your brother. You know that." His voice dropped to a whisper. "Don't make me say it."

"Say what?" I was whispering, too. The room smelled like flowery lotions and perfumes from some bottles that had burst open—girly creams he'd given me that I didn't value enough.

He looked at me. If I lied now, I'd lose him. But maybe that was best. Maybe I didn't deserve someone like him. "There's nothing to say, Daniel. It's just a hard time. I've been having a hard time."

He looked away from me with a slight nod, out the window. "Right." He drew a deep breath and started speaking, still looking out the window. "I remember the first time I saw you years ago at that seminar. I remember looking at you and listening to you and thinking, 'She's interesting. And she's really smart.' But I didn't think much else. Until the next day. I woke up and looked at the ceiling and I *knew* I had dreamed about you. I knew it. You had invaded my sleep." He laughed a little. "I remember looking at the ceiling and wondering what had happened. How you had gotten inside of me so fast." He looked at me for a long moment. "You're still there. But I that doesn't make everything all right."

Twenty-three

Tick hadn't been in Woods Hole more than a couple of weeks before he knew he was in trouble. He should have seen the trouble coming when he stood on that porch and I slapped him in the face. He should have seen the trouble coming when he just couldn't get himself to those AA meetings the very day he arrived. That nice kid had even told him where they were. But he didn't go. He was so tired. The bus ride had been so long. It was so good to sit on my porch drinking coffee and watching the birds fly by. He kept thinking of that kid's smile. The one in the coffee shop. He thought maybe remembering that would be enough.

He heard Daniel and me whispering fiercely to each other in our bedroom, in the study, in the kitchen, over and over, all the time. He heard his name sometimes in the midst of these whispers. Then he'd make a noisy show of entering the room and we'd stop talking and look at him guiltily and say a loud fakey, "Hi." Or "How are you doing? What do you need?"

We couldn't help him with what he really needed. What he was starting to feel like he needed. He was past all the sick feelings; that was the funny part. He'd ridden out the shakes, the nausea, the grinding in the bones. Now he just . . . missed it. Right under his heart was painful and tender. Raw. He didn't have that feeling when he was drunk or high.

He started taking long walks on the beach to try to take his mind off the wound. Being outside and moving around helped a bit. It made the aching subside, if not cease altogether. He wasn't sure how to outrun it. He thought he ought to talk to someone. But he was so tired of talking. Talking and fighting this thing with all that one-day-at-a-time crap was all he'd done for so long. He was so tired of it.

He ran into Ben on the beach during a very early morning walk—he was finding it harder and harder to sleep. Tick felt compelled to speak to him—he hadn't seen another black guy in days and days.

"Hey," he said.

"Hey," said the other guy. He was thin and dark-skinned,

bookish and thoughtful looking. "I never see people out this early. That's why I like to come out now."

"Yeah?" said Tick. "I just couldn't sleep. That's why I'm out here. Better than laying there, staring at the ceiling. Listen, I gotta introduce myself. There just ain't that many of us here. My name's Edmund," he said. "But everyone calls me Tick."

The guy took a step backward. Tick wondered if Josie had told everyone in town about her fuck-up brother. "So you're Tick," the other man said. "Nice to meet you."

"What do you mean, 'So you're Tick?' How do you know me, man?"

"Oh, sorry. My name's Ben Davidson. I work with your sister, Josie, at the lab. She mentioned you to me."

"Mmm." Tick nodded. They had fallen into step. "So you're the other one."

"Other what?" His voice climbed a little. Tick looked at him sharply. Ben had that look in his eye, that look a man gets about a woman. Well. Looked like Josie might have her own secrets. But he couldn't blame her; both he and his sister had their own hellhounds on their trail. And he did not want to step into her pile of shit. He had enough of his own.

So all Tick said was, "You're the only other black doc at the institute. She told me that there was one other black guy. She likes you." Tick couldn't resist this little dig, just to see what the guy would do. He held his ground, but the air between them shifted a little. Tick picked up a rock and slung it with unforced grace toward the ocean.

"What do you mean, she likes me?" Ben asked.

"She just said you were an all-right guy. That it was nice to have somebody else black around the office. You study fish, too, right?"

"I'm a marine biologist. Specialize in the life of plankton."

"Plankton, huh? Seems kind of hard to study that stuff. It's so small. Just all one big mush."

"Not exactly," Ben said uncertainly. "It's an ecosystem. Part of how everything in the ocean lives together."

"I know what an ecosystem is," Tick said testily. "I went to the same high school as Josie. I've got some education." Suddenly, Tick started coughing so hard that he had to stop walking and bend over, leaning on his thighs. Ben stopped with him and put his hand on Tick's back. It felt good to have another man's hand on his back in that friendly, caring way. He'd divorced himself from so many things, even warm regard from another man.

When he was able to stand he said, "Sorry, man. Sometimes this sea air gets to me, you know? Anyway, what are you doing out so early? I know why I can't sleep. Why can't you?"

Ben looked out at the water and narrowed his eyes.

"Sometimes I just can't sleep," he said after a while. "The ceiling starts pressing down on my head."

Tick nodded. "I know what you mean."

They both fell silent, walking along companionably. Until Tick banished the silence with his next words to Ben: "You wouldn't happen to have ten dollars I could borrow, man, would you?"

"What?"

"Ten dollars. You wouldn't happen to have it on you. Would you?"

Ben stepped away from Tick, shaking his head. He looked sad and sorry, like he'd seen something beautiful lying dead in the road. Tick felt like the lowest form of life there was. He couldn't even believe that those words had just come out of his mouth. And yet—he did want it. He needed it. He wasn't going to use it for booze. But still. He was a grown man. He hated walking around with no money, no nothing. Josie didn't trust him with anything.

"No, man. I don't have ten dollars. Not today. Not for you."

Tick felt a tight smile cross his face. "So she warned you, huh?"

"She said a little bit about you. But I think I'd have figured you out anyway."

Tick turned to head back. The camaraderie was gone.

He walked away and then started a loping run, trying to make it look casual, like what he had just done wasn't a big thing. Like it wasn't yet another defeat.

A COUPLE OF DAYS after that walk on the beach, Tick and I were sitting on my porch. Daniel was at work, finishing up a project. I had been able to get away to see Ben a couple of times but not often. And when I did? Well, let's just say it wasn't the same. But I wasn't ready to let go yet. There was still some comfort there. But for now, it was just me and Tick. There was between us, for the first time since he'd arrived, a little bit of ease. We both had our feet up on the railing, something we couldn't do when we were kids, partly because Mom and Daddy would have given us a good talking-to and partly because our feet wouldn't have reached the railing. We stared at the road, watching the occasional car pass by.

"I met Ben, that guy you work with," he said suddenly.

"What?"

He turned and gave me a slow look. He knew. How did he know? But I could tell he did, all in one electric moment. "He seems like a nice guy." He kept looking at me steadily. "Look, Josie, what you do is your business. You're grown. And God knows I am not in a position to tell anybody what to do. But I hope he's good to you." He paused. "And I hope you know what you're doing." He looked back out at the road.

I took a deep breath. "I'm not sure I do. But I can't stop." My eyes stung.

"Well, I know what that's like," he said. He reached over and took my hand. We sat quiet for a few minutes.

"What are you gonna do, Tick?"

"What do you mean, what am I gonna do?"

"Tick, you showed up on my doorstep strung out, no money, no job, no plan, no program. You're not even going to meetings."

"I hate meetings."

"You hate meetings," I said.

"Yeah, I do. You sit there with these people and they all talk about how we've got to rely on this higher power and how it's out of their hands and they tell these long-ass stories and then we all hold hands and say that damn prayer." He paused. "I want to kick by myself."

"You do."

"Yeah, I do. That's why I came up here. I thought if I could get away from all the craziness, it would be easier to kick. You know. You'd be here to help me, and it's nice and quiet."

"Not to mention that Mom threw your rusty butt into the street."

A car drove past, slowly, and Tick looked at it. A muscle worked in his throat. "I came up here to get straight. I came up here because I thought you and Daniel would take me in."

A long silence fell. I broke it. "Remember how you used to always sleep at the end of my bed when you were scared? You used to curl up right at my feet."

"Yeah, I remember."

"Tick, I'll do what I can for you but you've got to do this yourself. You know that, right?"

"I know."

"I'm scared for you."

"I can do it, Josie."

"I hope so."

We were quiet again, both of us looking out at the road, still holding hands, a couple of kids who had always trusted each other.

"I love you, Tick. You know that, right?"

"I know. I love you, too. I'll go to a meeting, Josie," he said. "I promise."

. . .

He was as good as his word. He went to a meeting the next night. He felt depressed and hopeless the minute he walked through the door. Those same stupid folding chairs. The same linoleum that they all seemed to have ordered from the same place in that same shade of yellowy green. The quiet hissing of the coffee maker, the murmuring of the people who knew each other already, the shell-shocked look of those who'd found themselves there for the first time and weren't ever, ever going to open their mouths. That's what they thought anyway. Tick remembered feeling that way. And he remembered how good at first it felt to give in to their embrace, to share at a meeting and feel supported and like someone finally got why it was so hard to quit using. He remembered the first time in rehab, the twice-a-day meetings, the bed making, the order, and how that all fell apart in a year when he got out. And then he went back. And then, he was out again. And then he was in a bar. And now he was here. Again. He knew, in his head anyway, that the whole idea was to keep putting one foot in front of the other and sticking with the program. But now? He couldn't remember exactly when he got the feeling that he might be beyond help. Was it this last run? Was it with that girl at Beenie's? When was it? The slogans—One Day at a Time, Think, Keep the Focus on Yourself, Zip the Lip—he couldn't remember exactly when it all started to get on his nerves, all that talk, all that serenity-seeking. When it started to be harder and harder to get himself to a meeting and stay in his seat while he was there. He couldn't remember when it began. But as soon as he sat down—in the back, where he'd most likely be left alone—nothing had changed. And he felt his heart tighten against whatever the room had to offer.

The speaker that night was a white woman. Maybe thirty-five, maybe forty. Honey-toned blond hair, nicely cut. She had a nervous habit of twirling her pretty hair around one finger as she talked. "So it started like this," she said. And the drunkalogue began. People laughed and nodded. The night she couldn't remember where she parked her car. The night she woke up fifty miles from home in the arms of a total stranger. The night she cut off all her hair. The night she drove her best friend's kids' home and barely avoided causing a major accident and killing herself and them. The thousands of times she prayed for deliverance. The way that she began to be delivered when she gave it all over. Her finger kept twisting her hair, mesmerizingly. Her voice rose and fell like a song. Everyone laughed at the funny parts. Everyone sighed as the story got sadder. Everyone knew how it ended. "So here's how it is now," she said. "I still look at those bottles of white wine in the grocery store. They look so cool and inviting. There are always those beads of moisture on them, you know? They look so great." A few nods. "But then I remember what happened after the first drink. Thank God for cell phones!" she laughed. She told of how she had called her sponsor and she'd talked her off the ledge. Everyone laughed with her. Tick didn't laugh. His legs hurt. He wanted a drink. He wanted a drink more than he had ever wanted anything in his life. He wanted that cold, clear savor, that cold, clear savior. He wanted to be saved. But he didn't think that what was in this room was going to save him.

The share finished. The treasury envelope made its way around the room. Tick shuffled his feet, shifted around in his chair, was acutely aware of being the only black person in the room. He got up and got some coffee. He sat back down. He stretched his back. Everyone laughed again at something someone said. Now someone said a slogan. Now heads were nodding; a young woman wept quietly in the corner. People talked about how their lives were saved, how hard they worked, how grace had come into their lives through those rooms. Tick tried to sit still. He tried to feel grace. It had worked for his father. For his own father. But all he could feel was the wind whistling through his heart. That sore, empty space that he'd tried so hard, so often, so long to fill. The meeting finally ended—it felt as though it had lasted a thousand years. He left without speaking to anyone. He folded up his chair and put it away like he was supposed to so he wouldn't call attention to himself. He went outside and stood alone under the brilliant stars.

He went to the Captain Kidd right from the meeting. What was the point of trying? This was what he wanted. No more slogans. The beer tasted like mother's milk, like everything he'd ever wanted. He could hear cars passing, other drinkers behind him in the bar, the Red Hot Chili Peppers on the jukebox. This was what he wanted. This was all he wanted. This was what would make everything all right.

He drank for a long time. He drank until the buzzing in his head seemed to stop and the hole in his chest was patched. He drank until his hands were steady again. He drank until the money he'd stolen from the jar in the kitchen where Daniel and I kept spare cash was gone. When he left the bar, the stars overhead were screaming. He could hear them. Tiny individual voices, all crying out in pain. Who said the stars were beautiful? Whoever said there was any point to a black velvet night? He stumbled off the stool, across the road, and out onto a pier that wasn't far away.

When he got there, the screaming in his head was louder. The waves barely masked it. Their constant rhythm was not a comfort. Nothing could comfort him now. There was all this screaming in his ears. He was never going to get what he needed. Never. He took his shoes off and threw them into the water. He was crying, he supposed. But why shouldn't he be? Why wasn't everybody? Drunk's tears. Everyone should weep them. He walked toward the end of the pier, furiously pulling off his clothes as he walked. The air was hot, sitting on him, a damp weight. And now, here, again, here, his sister couldn't save him, his mother couldn't save him, his father couldn't save him, no one could save him. What was there to be saved? He was stripped down to his underwear now, at the end of the pier. He jumped off, into the freezing water. A baptism at last. He gasped and bobbed up and began to swim out, away from land. He didn't know what he wanted. He only wanted to stop asking. He only wanted to stop needing to know. Water flowed into his mouth. The salt was bitter; nausea took him the next few feet. He vomited but it wasn't wrenching. Not the way it usually was when he was really fucked up. Not the way it was on land. He kicked away from the foul traces he left in the water; he was sorry for that. To have fouled the ocean as he fouled the land, as he fouled everything he touched. He hung in the water's embrace, holding his breath, treading for a moment. But he wasn't going back. Soon he would be too tired. He wouldn't have the strength to get back to land. He just didn't have the strength. For a moment, he was glad he didn't have any children. *I'm sorry, Josie. I'm sorry.* That was his last thought. And then he gave in. There was no reason to resist anymore. One day at a time, he had arrived at his last end.

Twenty-four

When the phone rang, I hadn't been sleeping long. Given the events of the last few days, it's a miracle I was sleeping at all. There was what Daniel had said to me about leaving. I could tell by the silence he maintained around me that he meant it. And Ben. After that last time, the day after Tick arrived, I'd felt him receding away from me even faster, even farther. And I knew, in my core, in my gut, that I had to let go of him, too. Oh, and of course my alcoholic, drug-addicted brother was sleeping on my sofa and not doing much else by the looks of it. Well, really, who had time? Who had time to sleep? I was being eaten alive by men, by their needs and their vague insanities. Not that I was doing that much better with my own needs and vague insanities. I wasn't. Don't think I didn't know that. But still. I felt oppressed by the weight of them. The phone ringing in the darkest part of the night was just another imposition. Probably another man on the line. A man who needed something. I picked up the phone.

"Yes?"

"Is this Ms. Josie Henderson?"

My breath got short. This was a very official voice. The voice of doom. "Yes it is."

"Ms. Henderson, there's been an accident. We need you to come down to the hospital."

Daniel was here. No one would call me if something happened to Ben. Tick. It had to be Tick. He hadn't come home after the meeting. I had been frightened but wanted to give him some space, too. He had to work this out on his own. I swallowed hard, once. "Who's involved?"

"Please just come down to the hospital, ma'am. We'll be able to explain more here."

I hung up the phone and sat up. Abruptly, I had to vomit. I ran clumsily into the bathroom. By the time I returned to the bed, Daniel was sitting up, pulling on his pants. "It's Tick, isn't it?" he said.

I nodded. Who else could it be? What else could it be? I went to the drawer and pulled out some clothing. I put my shirt on inside out, as I recall. I don't know why I remember that kind of detail. But I do. The kitchen smelled faintly of rotting cantaloupe. I remember that, too. I'd had some for breakfast and it had been a hot day and no one took the trash out. I was briefly afraid I would vomit again.

Daniel drove. Even with all that had been going on, the ways I hid from him, the ways I'd betrayed him, he was still my husband, still the one to drive the car in a situation like this. Using his turn signal carefully. Looking up into the rearview mirror with the same slight scowl he always had when he looked in the rearview mirror. Silence lay between us like a body. There was nothing safe to talk about. "Danny?"

He didn't look away from the road. "Yeah?"

"I'm scared." The first true words I'd said to him for a while.

That made him look at me briefly. His eyes were gentle and considering—a look that hadn't been directed my way for some time. "I'm scared, too, Jose. This whole thing scares the shit out of me."

I looked back out the front window. I couldn't say any more. We would be at the hospital soon.

Here I was pulling up to another institution. Here I was for my brother again. I tripped getting out of the car. Daniel caught my elbow and kept me from falling. We walked into the hospital with our sides almost touching. But not quite.

The hospital smelled like hospital. Blood, rubbing alcohol, sadness. It reminded me a little bit of the lab—I found the smell of the alcohol rather comforting. But at work there isn't the salty odor of people sweating and crying. The sharp tang of despair. We went up to the desk, gave them our names. The shift nurse pressed her lips together and spoke into her telephone. We were ushered to seats.

After a short while, a tired-looking doctor came out. He couldn't have been more than twenty-seven or twenty-eight. He was Indian and he had a slight accent. "Please, Mrs. . . ?"

"Henderson. I didn't change my name. This is my husband, Daniel Ehrmann." Why did I explain all that? What did this young doctor care?

He nodded. "Come with me."

We followed him down a quiet corridor. At an unmarked door, he turned and spoke. "I must tell you, the news I have is not good. I'm very sorry. He was found washed up in the cove just before dawn this morning. It appears to have been a simple drowning. By the time he was brought here, it was too late." He lowered his head as though it really saddened him. "We found his driver's license with his clothing and notified the next of kin in Ohio. Your mother, I believe. She told us that he was here staying with you." I looked at the floor. So Mom knew already. The young doctor was still talking. "The police have been notified but this seems a simple matter. Though a sad one." My knees gave out.

Daniel put his arm around me and led me to a lonely chair in the corridor and knelt beside me. The young doctor stood quietly a few feet away, silent. But after a few minutes, he spoke again. "I'll need you to come identify the body."

I looked up at him. The body. What was left of Tick. All that was left of my only brother. I suddenly felt as though my bones were full of tar, as though I would never, never rise from this seat again. Daniel stood. He brought me to my feet, his hand never losing contact with the planes of muscle on my back, willing to touch me again at last. We walked through the door together, the doctor leading the way.

No one had died on me before. This is something of a miracle, but it is also a fact. I've seen many dead fish and sea mammals, but I had never looked at a dead human face, the face of someone I loved. I had spent my life studying the life all around us in the water. I had spent my life sifting it through my fingers and considering the light, thin bones. I had spent my life this way, considering how the life all around us passes away. And now I would see it in a face I'd always known.

It was like the TV shows. The doctor had a careful look on his face. He pulled out a drawer, not unlike the filing system we use for our samples. Neat and clean and careful. Nothing messy here. I could hear my own breath, the drip of water from the slop sink. The drawer pulled out noiselessly. The face covered, the body an undifferentiated mass. The doctor didn't say anything, just pulled the sheet back. There he was.

A sound came out of me that I didn't know I could make. Halfway between a scream and a moan. Daniel made a startled gasp. Tick's chin was pointed to the ceiling, his beautiful brown skin ash-colored and rubbery. His eyes were closed; I suppose someone had done that here. They had probably been open when they brought him in. I touched his shoulder. It was cold. The kind of cold you know you'll never forget. I pulled my fingers away quickly. The room smelled of formaldehyde and alcohol, a familiar smell. "That's him. That's my brother."

The doctor spoke again. "Is there anything that you'd want the authorities to know?"

He was my brother. He couldn't stop drinking, no matter how hard he tried, even though my father managed to stop. We used to do everything together. We were always together. "No. He'd had some substance-abuse problems. He was up here trying to get away from all that. I'm sure that something just went wrong."

The doctor nodded. Pulled the sheet back up. "There

will be some paperwork." I nodded. "Do you two need a few more minutes?"

"Could we?" This from Daniel. The doctor left without another word.

We stood alone in the freezing room. "Daniel?"

He was still looking fixedly at Tick's face. I said his name again and he looked up.

"What do we do now?"

He sighed. "We go home," he said. "I'll help you through this. But what I said the other day . . . it still goes."

There was nothing I could say about anything at all. So after a long minute, looking at my disappearing husband over my brother's dead body, I said, "Okay." I wiped at my wet cheeks. I looked at Tick's shell for another long moment. "We'd better go out there and find out what we have to do next," I said. He nodded and we walked out of the room together. I felt as though someone was stabbing me in the chest. Ben gone, Daniel gone, Tick gone. I was all alone. I bit my lip. And there was so much to do. Daniel and I didn't say anything else. The only words left were official ones.

Twenty-five

My name is Ray and I'm an alcoholic. When my son, Tick, was a baby, I never fed him. I left that job to my wife. In those days, the man hardly ever did anything for the baby. That's what we all thought was how it should be. I wasn't drinking too much then, not yet. Or really, it wasn't out of hand yet. I guess that was the thing. I could still handle my liquor. It wasn't handling me. But even so, I'd look at that little brown boy in his crib, that little brown baby, that little bit of life that our love had made, and I felt so uncertain. I didn't know what to do with him. Even though he was our second, he was so much harder. He cried so much and seemed to want so much and we could hardly ever figure out what he wanted.

I still remember how his body felt pressed against mine when I picked him up. Warm and moving against me, that beautiful smell their heads have, those tiny curls pressed against my mouth. I can remember those anytime I like. Those little beads of hair so soft against my lips.

Sarah thought she knew what was best for him. But in the end, she didn't know what to do either. And she never would take any help—even after I moved out and cleaned up and started with the meetings, she wouldn't go. Said she'd be all right on her own. She never wanted to ask for anything. I remember, first time I saw her at Leo's Casino, I noticed that about her. She was all to herself. Everything she needed was inside her. When I looked at her, I thought I'd get what I needed, too. I was already feeling that hole. When she couldn't fill it, well, I had to keep looking.

Before the kids came and before everything went bad, before the bottle got out in front of me and we lost all that time, we used to lie in bed spooned together and I knew that everything would be all right as long as our skin could rest together like that. It seemed like the kind of thing that would never end, that should never end, that could never end. Her hip against mine like that. Those were the best times I was ever to know. In the bars, at first, I thought those were the best times. But they didn't last. And the pleasures they offered were hollow in the end. Wasn't long before I couldn't even remember what happened from one bar to the next. Those times lying next to my Sarah, angel that she was, ministering to me, those were the best times I was ever to know. And I threw them away like so much garbage.

Well, my mama used to say there would be a reckoning. And I guess when Tick died, that was mine. Josie was the one who had to call me. My poor girl. I never gave her nothing but sorrow either. And now here she was, calling me to tell me that her brother killed himself on her watch. I never heard a woman sound as broken as she sounded on that phone.

I was sitting in the apartment, watching TV when the phone rang. I had a Coke beside me. That had been one of the hardest times to give up the beer, in front of the TV. Coke was a little like it, the bubbles, the cold. But it was sweet and lacked that sharp edge and—well, I'd be a damn lie if I didn't say I miss the beer sometimes. But I call my sponsor and I drink my Coke and I get past those moments. I go on. The day Josie called about Tick, I wasn't even thinking about it. It was one of those days I wasn't missing the beer. I felt fine.

So when I heard my daughter's voice for the first time in

a while, first time in months—years maybe—that she had called me, not me calling her. I thought it was definitely on its way to being a good day. I was so happy until she said enough that I could catch the tone of her voice.

So she told me. She told me that she was going to have to fly my son, her brother's body, home. She told me my boy was dead.

You know, the first thing I thought after she told me was that this was the call I sometimes thought someone would have to make about me before I got sober. There were nights when I wished to God that someone *would* have to make that call, that I'd be out of my misery. I didn't think about the misery I would have left behind. I'd caused so much pain already. What was a little bit more?

Josie said some more things. I suppose I must have responded somehow, said something. Plane tickets. Arrangements. What would happen next. We must have talked about all that. But all I could think was that my boy was dead. My boy was dead. My boy was dead and I couldn't save him. Hell. I probably half helped kill him. Not supposed to think like that anymore. But I couldn't help but think that for a moment. What's my part in this? I had a part. I played it so wrong for so long. And now my boy was dead. I looked out the window. It was dark out. People were walking places. I threw my can of Coke against the wall. It splattered and left a dark brown mark I would have to clean. So this was what a broken heart felt like. I thought I knew. Turned out I didn't. Now I knew for sure.

Twenty-six

The last time he kissed her, he knew it would be the last time he kissed her. There was too much between them now—too much pain, too much longing, too many things that neither of them could heal in the other. He found himself noting things about that kiss, the temperature of her lips, her smell. Though their parting was always going to happen, he hadn't expected it to be so sudden, so without long conversations. She was just gone like so much smoke.

The last time he saw her, it was very early morning. He'd opened the door, a garbage bag in his hand, and there she was. Just standing there. Bedraggled and breathing rapidly, her face tear-stained.

Josie?

Ben? My brother's dead. My brother killed himself. He's dead. He drowned. She looked right into his eyes as she said this last.

That was the moment when the end became inevitable. He felt himself slipping away from her, even as he lowered himself onto the sofa next to her. Oh my God, Josie. Really?

She nodded miserably. He pulled her to him. Already her body felt a little strange, a little distant. After a while, she shifted a little and he lowered his mouth to hers. Not to have her, not to fuck her or taste her or swallow her. Just to offer some warmth to someone he had once cared about very deeply. She tasted of bitter orange sorrow.

They kissed for a while, but she didn't want much else either. Just to be held and desired outside of the hard things she now had to face. She talked a lot. She talked of how much she had loved Tick and the things they'd done together as children. She talked of the time that "Start Me Up" came on the radio and she was in her room and Tick was in his room and they both burst out at the same moment, dancing joyously in the upstairs hallway to the same song on their little radios. She smiled a little at that memory. She talked and talked and he sat there with his arm around her and gradually it was as if she were a beloved sister herself. Not entirely. What had gone on between them wasn't completely gone—all the flesh and the heat, all the desire and the smacking together—he didn't want to deny all that. But it was not the important thing any longer. Not for him. And, it seemed, not for her.

After a while, she fell silent. Morning had turned to afternoon. Neither of them knew how long they'd sat there.

Are you hungry? he asked her.

I am a little, she said. Seems funny to eat with him gone. But I have to.

Neither of them said a word about her husband. Where he was, why she was with Ben at this moment. He gave her bread and butter, cold bacon, sardines from an opened can in the fridge—the eccentric foods of a man who lived alone and didn't like to cook. She ate them without comment. She looked at him steadily as she ate. After a while she said, There's things I have to do. I'd better go. He nodded. He kissed her again, his hand on the small of her back, her tongue warm and eager inside his mouth. He tried to put everything into that kiss, to tell her he did love her but not in a way that was useful, that could live. His love couldn't save her. She was going to have to save herself. When she pulled away, her eyes were full of tears. Right, she said. And she turned and left without another word. After the door closed behind her, he finally spoke. Take care of yourself, Josie, is what he said.

Twenty-seven

When a man dies the way Tick did, everyone staggers around, bumping into each other, not knowing what to do. I went home because, of course, I had to. Somebody had to fly his body home. I had to be there when he was laid to rest. Tick needed to lay his head down in Cleveland, not in Woods Hole. I spoke to my mother a few times. Her voice sounded drowned, just like Tick's body, buried under gallons and gallons of salt water. "The unplumb'd, salt, estranging sea." I read that sentence in *The French Lieutenant's Woman,* one of the few novels I've ever read on my own. I'd seen the movie on TV and liked it and my father gave me the book, eager to encourage me to read fiction. I read it at a time when I was desperate for distraction.

Someone had broken up with me, someone I loved very much, though he was unworthy of that love. I never forgot those words. The sea was never estranging to me. It was on land that I had my difficulties, my lack of comprehension, my estrangement. But something about all those *s*'s all together, the hiss of them, I knew even as I read them that they'd come back to me someday. And here they were again.

And my father. Gone from the house for so long. Gone from me for so long. I had ended it with him. In my mind. My heart. I had just ended it. I knew he'd quit drinking for good, and to hear my mother tell it, he was different. Quieter, where he'd always been quiet. But now there was someone there in all the silence. Sometimes she made a shy reference to a dinner out with him, something he said that had made her laugh. But I didn't care. I just remembered him sitting in front of the TV. Slumped in jockey shorts. What was on? Did it matter? It never seemed to matter. It was just always on, always talking, that TV, and him, sullen, silent, with a beer in his hand. Sometimes there would be anger, always a rumble, never a hurricane blast. But the looking at me, at us, and seeing us, the actual us, there? There was none of that either. He was just a presence. Or really, more of a terrifying lack of a presence.

That made it feel especially strange that he was the one who met me at the airport. I wasn't used to him showing up for me anywhere. Daniel was with me, too, but that was all splintering, breaking, falling away like so much dust. There had been too much damage. I had done too much damage. He didn't ask any questions; I offered no answers. He read a monograph the whole flight. I stared out the window. I knew I would be moving out when we got back to Woods Hole. He stood a few steps behind me as we got off the plane.

My father stood at the gate, wearing the same kind of flat-brimmed cap he always did, the kind you see only on black men of his generation and a little older. The kind that black men who call people "cat" with ease wear. Sometimes it's herringbone plaid, sometimes it's black. It's never seen comfortably sitting on the head of a white man. Old-school rappers wore puffy ones made of some furry material. And men my father's age who still wear that exact kind are dying out. But there are still a few. There is still my father.

His skin and eyes were clear. He stood up straight. He was the man he'd been for years, the man I refused to see. And when he took me in his arms, which he did without hesitation, he smelled good and clean and present. I had never accepted a real hug from him; I didn't believe he could offer them. But I was wrong. And now I wasn't strong enough to resist. I was surprised at the comfort it gave me, to be held by my father, whom I am supposed to love, but so often fear that I don't. We stood embracing for a long time. I felt held. I felt something very small and hard begin to unknot. But I didn't cry. Daniel stood behind us, a fatherless boy, a wifeless man, outside the circle. My father let me go after a few minutes and turned to him. He held Daniel just as he had held me, and Daniel, the one who is not his child, broke down completely. I had to turn away. It didn't last long but it was as if he were crying for all of us.

Daniel finally lifted his head, abashed. My father handed him his cotton handkerchief calmly, without embarrassment or fuss, and allowed him to wipe at his face. He turned away from Daniel. "Well, baby girl. I think we'd better go on home. Your mother's in kind of a state over this." He paused. "All our hearts are broken. I wish to God I could have done something to help that boy. My boy." His gaze was steady and clear. He extended his hand and I took it.

MY STREET NEVER CHANGES. Sometimes there are FOR SALE signs. Sometimes there aren't. But the houses always look the same, new generations of light- and dark-skinned kids riding their bikes in wavering lines over the pebbly sidewalks. The lawns green and small and carefully tended, each blade full of hope, except for the one or two houses where folks have just given up. No one ever says anything to them, but everybody talks about those folks. Daniel wasn't with us. My father said he thought it would be best if my mother just saw me at first so he dropped Daniel off at the hotel. As we pulled up to my old house, I saw that our lawn, my mother's pride and joy, had become one of those lawns. The tussocky grass was nearly ankle-high, the garden running riot. My poor mother.

My father pulled the car in carefully and all but took my elbow as I got out of the car, treating me carefully, like glass. He walked next to me going to the porch, his presence steady. "Josie," he said as I approached the door, "you need to be ready for how she's going to be."

"How is she?"

"Pretty bad, Josie. I'm not so good myself but I've found some ways to get through. I've been going to a lot of meetings. But you know how your mother was about Tick." He reached down to unlock the door, then straightened back up and looked at me. He put his hands on my shoulders. "Are you okay?"

"As okay as I can be, Daddy." My father, the rock in a storm? A fount of wisdom? My father? What was going on? I sure wished Tick could see this. That thought made me wince. It hurt to have him come rushing into my mind, to want to tell him something, and not be able to.

"Daddy?"

"Yes, baby girl."

"Daddy, I don't know if I can do this."

"I know, baby girl. I know it's hard. But come on. Let's go in."

All the shades were drawn and the house smelled of sweat and garbage. It was dead silent at first and then I heard some sobbing. The same as the night she called me about Tick. I stopped walking so abruptly that my father bumped into me.

"Daddy, what am I supposed to do?"

"You go on up there and be with her, that's what you're supposed to. Just sit by the bed and be with her. She needs her daughter to be with her now. I'll be right down here."

Panic rose up in me. I climbed the stairs like a child entering a forest.

The shades were drawn in Mom's room. It was cool and dark. It had an unexpected undersea feeling that I found slightly comforting. She lay in bed, smaller than she used to be.

"Mom? Mom, it's me. I came to see you. I'm here."

Her head lifted up from the pillow where it lay but her eyes were far gone, ranging off to some other shore, some land we couldn't see. "Josie. Josie, you came home."

"Yes, Mom."

"Where's Tick? He must be out. He'll be glad to see you."

I thought I might bite through my lip before I spoke. "Tick's dead, Mom. Remember? He's dead."

She closed her eyes and lowered her head back onto the pillow. She nodded slowly.

"I miss him a lot." And when I said the words, they came true, took on flesh and body and life. He was my brother and now he was gone. I sat down heavily on the edge of the bed. "I know you miss him, too, Mom. The way he used to be."

"The way he used to be," she said uncertainly.

"Yeah, you know, before everything . . ."

"My baby boy." Her voice cracked. "You know, when he came home this time, when he first came home, he was so sweet and so hopeful. We laughed. We laughed together those first couple of months. You know how he was, Josie. I'd be watching something on television and he'd come and sit with me and say some silly stuff and we'd just laugh and laugh. I think that's when I first knew things were starting to go bad. When he stopped coming to me and making me laugh." She couldn't talk anymore. She covered her face and started crying again.

Without thinking, I leaned over her on the bed and embraced her with my full length. I hadn't held her like that since I was little. I could feel her skin and her muscle and all her bones moving within her. I felt her shoulders heaving as she cried. I cried, too. All you could hear was the sound of our sadness.

AND THEN LATER, THERE was the crying, the shock, the relatives and friends saying, "Oh, I remember when." There I was, standing in the backyard where our climbing structure used to be, looking up at the stark blue and white sky, remembering how Tick used to fly down the sidewalk on his bike. There were whispered caucuses with Daniel and the knowledge that I was no longer married to him and that when I got back Ben would no longer be my lover. I was all alone.

The day Daniel and I were married, after the ceremony, after everyone went home, we went swimming. The beach was deserted. We took off our clothes and laid them in piles in the sand, my going-away dress a bright spill of orange. I remember the shock of the water, how it felt to see his pale body and know it belonged to me now. I remember how the water felt all over me, a baptism. After we buried Tick, I wanted that again. I didn't tell anyone. I just took the car and drove over to Lake Erie very, very early one morning. It would have to do.

It was a beautiful day. Not too warm, but not too cold. Despite the lovely weather, no one was around. My brother's body was beneath the earth, in the same city he'd been born in. I took off my jacket, my shoes, my dress and left them on the rocky shore. I waded into the lake, knees, thighs, chest, shoulders. I lowered my head to receive the water and swam. It was just a lake. No salt. No majesty. A gentle rocking of waves. It was where I was born, this lake, this cold gray nothing special. I stroked out for a long way, then floated a little, and then, chilled, swam back to the shore. My mind was blank.

There was someone standing near my clothes. Not much taller than me, dark skin. My father. He didn't look surprised to see me naked. And I was too heartbroken to be afraid or embarrassed. He looked at me unsmiling as I emerged dripping. He was wearing his hard shoes, just as he always had at the beach. He picked up my dress and held it out for me. I climbed into it the same way I might have if I were at home alone, no anxiety, no modesty. He didn't say anything while I dressed.

"I thought you might be down here," he said.

"Yes," I said. "You know I love the water, Daddy."

We both turned to face it and he put one arm around my shivering shoulders.

"You're not alone," he said.

"Yes, I am," I said. "I am." He turned me to face him, a little roughly. He looked into my eyes harder than he ever had in his whole life. Every bit of my father was in that look.

Every inch of him that I had never been willing to see before. He had been restored. He had done what was necessary. He wasn't the man I never knew.

"You're not alone anymore," he said. "I'm your father and I'm right here. You're not alone anymore."

He pulled me toward him and held me for a long minute. I let go first. We stood side by side looking at the small sibilant waves. Then he took off his shoes and his socks and led me back to the edge and we stood there and let the water bathe our feet. He said it again. "You're not alone anymore. Do you believe me?"

I didn't speak. I offered a small nod. He squeezed my hand. "I'm here when you want me, baby," he said. "I'm here." I nodded. We stood there holding hands, gazing at the muddy greenish waves together.

ACKNOWLEDGMENTS

Charles Baxter, Joanne Gruber, Sharon Guskin, Anne Rumsey, and my husband, Jeff Phillips, all provided tremendous help and thoughtful comments in their readings of one or several of the many drafts of this novel.

My agent, Geri Thoma, who has stood by my work, lo, these many years, always with enthusiasm and encouragement.

My editor, Jane Rosenman, provided wise counsel, skillful editing, and good cheer, as always.

Radford Arrindell of the American Museum of Natural History provided valuable insight into a scientist's life and an ichthyologist's work in particular (though Josie ended up being a marine biologist).

I believe I've thanked the MacDowell Colony at the end of each of my novels—but I'll keep doing it as long as I am allowed to spend time writing at this little bit of heaven. I can't ever express how helpful my residencies there have always been.

To Jeff, Nate, and Ruby: I am so fortunate to have you as my family.

To everyone named here and anyone who helped me along the way whom I've forgotten to name, I am and will always be deeply grateful.

The Taste of Salt

The Birth of *The Taste of Salt*

Questions for Discussion

The Birth of The Taste of Salt

BY MARTHA SOUTHGATE

The first inkling of what grew into *The Taste of Salt* developed when I was the books editor of *Essence* magazine, many years ago. A colleague's husband had what I thought was the coolest job I'd ever heard of. He was (and is) an ichthyologist (a scientist who specializes in the study of fish) at the American Museum of Natural History. Though I have no scientific background, I have always loved the water and could not stop thinking about how I might make the ocean and someone who loved it part of my next novel—I had already published one, *The Fall of Rome,* by that time. Though the novel took a long and winding road away from that initial inspiration, that is where it began.

When I began work on the book in earnest, all I had was that notion and the beginnings of the voice of my protagonist, Josie Henderson, a headstrong woman who loves the water and has fought her way into this white-male-dominated field. As I spent time with her, I came to feel that I wanted to write about where she came from, what made her tick, and what made her run. And I wanted her to be from Cleveland, my hometown.

Cleveland has always gotten a hard way to go in pop culture—"the mistake on the lake," the hapless sports teams, the disappearing industries. And yet, it's a place where hundreds of thousands of people live, love, make their lives and their homes. I have to admit that like Josie, when I left there, I swore I wasn't ever going back. But I had Cleveland be her hometown, too, because even though you might not go home again, you can't ever fully leave where you're from. The need to run is a big part of Josie's character, something I began to work out in the very earliest days of working on the novel. While working on this essay, I found some notes that I made in 2005 when I was thinking about how the novel might develop: "This story is about her heedlessness, her desire to let go of whatever's near her, her efforts to keep herself in control . . . She's scared and uncertain and a little wild."

And here's another note from that same page or two

of rumination, the birth of the other major theme of the book: "One big change today—have her go home and find out her brother's an addict. Parents flipping out. That's what she has to deal with when she gets home. Getting him into rehab or something. No sick dad. Let dad live and be present. Two parents. Crazy. And maybe we can build the marital conflict by rolling back through it. Let her relationship with her parents reflect her discomfort with her heritage, her hometown." Then I have a note to myself to begin researching "fish, addiction, water-related jobs." That's how it started, that one thought one day.

I've long been interested in the mechanisms and effects of addiction, but when I began work on this book, I had no idea it would become such a central theme. But that's what's great about writing fiction, the mystery of it, even as you do it. Eudora Welty once said, "If you haven't surprised yourself, you haven't written." Those words are part of why I write fiction, to attempt to surprise readers—and myself—with some aspect of story, some aspect of life, that they didn't expect to find. I hope that readers of *The Taste of Salt* will find themselves surprised and moved. I hope that they will find themselves thinking of how one lives in a family in a slightly different way.

Questions for Discussion

1. Josie, the protagonist of *The Taste of Salt,* is deeply tied to two places: Cleveland, Ohio, her birthplace, and Woods Hole, where she makes her life and work. She has very different relationships to each place. Discuss the ways in which the two places differ from one another. To what extent do they function as characters in the novel?

2. Josie's father, Ray, and her brother, Tick, both struggle with alcoholism and other addictions. Does Josie harbor any addictions of her own?

3. While there is alcoholism in the African-American community, as in any other community in the United States, relatively few memoirs or novels have been published about it. Why do you think that might be the case?

4. The author uses an interweaving narrative in which each of the six major characters speaks periodically and Josie serves as a kind of overarching consciousness going in and out of various characters' lives. Other novels that have taken this approach to a greater or lesser degree in recent years are Jeffrey Eugenides' *Middlesex* and Junot Díaz's *The Brief Wondrous Life of Oscar Wao*. Why do you think Southgate uses this narrative approach?

5. Josie struggles with both the family she came from and with conflicting feelings about being one of the only black scientists in her milieu. Why might successful people try to leave their past (and their families) behind? Do you think it's ever possible to do that?

6. On page 130, Josie says that she doesn't want to "fit the stereotype of black girl with a no 'count brother." Do you think there is such a stereotype? What do you think of Josie's comment or of the way it bonds her to her friend Maren?

7. The characters in the Henderson family have wildly varying reactions to the culture and tenets of Alcoholics Anonymous. What do you think of their range of responses? Are you familiar with the organization? If you are, what are your feelings about it?

8. *The Taste of Salt* is very much a story of family shame and acceptance. Does Tick ever arrive at that state of acceptance? Does Josie? Ray? Sarah?

9. What impact do you think race has on the alcoholism of the addicted characters in the novel?

10. If Josie had been able to make a life with Ben, do you think it would have been successful or would it have failed? Why? What do you think of her adulterous behavior?

11. How does the author portray her alcoholic characters—sympathetically or unsympathetically? How do those portrayals affect how we feel about everyone in the family?

12. When the author is from the same town as the protagonist, the tendency is to assume autobiography. What is gained and what is lost when the reader makes this assumption? How does it alter, enrich, or diminish your experience of the work?

13. At the novel's end, there is a strong sense of hope for a kind of reconciliation between father and daughter. What do you think would have to happen to make this a lasting reconciliation? Are you convinced by Ray's change in behavior and lifestyle? Do you think it's harder for women to make peace with deeply flawed mothers or deeply flawed fathers?

TOM RAWE

MARTHA SOUTHGATE is the author of three acclaimed previous novels, most recently *The Fall of Rome* and *Third Girl from the Left,* and other works that have been widely anthologized. She has written for *Essence, Premiere,* the *New York Daily News,* and the *New York Times.* A graduate of Smith College, she has an MFA in creative writing from Goddard and has taught at Brooklyn College and the New School. She lives in Brooklyn with her husband and two children.

Other Algonquin Readers Round Table Novels

A Friend of the Family, a novel by Lauren Grodstein

Pete Dizinoff has a thriving medical practice in suburban New Jersey, a devoted wife, a network of close friends, an impressive house, and a son, Alec, now nineteen, on whom he's pinned all his hopes. But Pete never counted on Laura, his best friend's daughter, setting her sights on his only son. Lauren Grodstein's riveting novel charts a father's fall from grace as he struggles to save his family, his reputation, and himself.

"Suspense worthy of Hitchcock . . . [Grodstein] is a terrific storyteller." —*The New York Times Book Review*

An Algonquin Readers Round Table Edition with Reading Group Guide and Other Special Features • Fiction • ISBN 978-1-61620-017-6

The Girl Who Fell from the Sky, a novel by Heidi W. Durrow

In the aftermath of a family tragedy, a biracial girl must cope with society's ideas of race and class in this acclaimed novel, winner of the Bellwether Prize for fiction addressing issues of social justice.

"Affecting, exquisite . . . Durrow's powerful novel is poised to find a place among classic stories of the American experience." —*The Miami Herald*

"Like *Catcher in the Rye* or *To Kill a Mockingbird,* Durrow's debut features voices that will ring in the ears long after the book is closed." —*The Denver Post*

Winner of the Bellwether Prize for Fiction

An Algonquin Readers Round Table Edition with Reading Group Guide and Other Special Features • Fiction • ISBN 978-1-61620-015-2

Pictures of You, a novel by Caroline Leavitt

Two women running away from their marriages collide on a foggy highway. The survivor of the fatal accident is left to pick up the pieces not only of her own life but of the lives of the devastated husband and fragile son that the other woman left behind. As these three lives intersect, the book asks, How well do we really know those we love and how do we open our hearts to forgive the unforgivable?

"An expert storyteller . . . Leavitt teases suspense out of the greatest mystery of all—the workings of the human heart."
—*Booklist*

"Magically written, heartbreakingly honest . . . Caroline Leavitt is one of those fabulous, incisive writers you read and then ask yourself, Where has she been all my life?" —Jodi Picoult

An Algonquin Readers Round Table Edition with Reading Group Guide and Other Special Features • Fiction • ISBN 978-1-56512-631-2

The Ghost at the Table, a novel by Suzanne Berne

When Frances arranges to host Thanksgiving at her idyllic New England farmhouse, she envisions a happy family reunion, one that will include her estranged sister, Cynthia. But as Thanksgiving Day arrives, the tension between Frances and Cynthia mounts, as each struggles with a different version of the mysterious circumstances surrounding their mother's death twenty-five years earlier.

"Wholly engaging, the perfect spark for launching a rich conversation around your own table."
—*The Washington Post Book World*

"A crash course in sibling rivalry." —*O: The Oprah Magazine*

An Algonquin Readers Round Table Edition with Reading Group Guide and Other Special Features • Fiction • ISBN 978-1-56512-579-7

In the Time of the Butterflies, a novel by Julia Alvarez

In this extraordinary novel, the voices of Las Mariposas (The Butterflies), Minerva, Patria, María Teresa, and Dedé, speak across the decades to tell their stories about life in the Dominican Republic under General Rafael Leonidas Trujillo's dictatorship. Through the art and magic of Julia Alvarez's imagination, the martyred butterflies live again in this novel of valor, love, and the human cost of political oppression.

A National Endowment for the Arts Big Read selection

"A gorgeous and sensitive novel . . . A compelling story of courage, patriotism, and familial devotion." —*People*

"A magnificent treasure for all cultures and all time." —*St. Petersburg Times*

An Algonquin Readers Round Table Edition with Reading Group Guide and Other Special Features • Fiction • ISBN 978-1-56512-976-4

How the García Girls Lost Their Accents,
a novel by Julia Alvarez

In Julia Alvarez's brilliant and buoyant first novel, the García sisters, newly arrived from the Dominican Republic, tell their most intimate stories about how they came to be at home—and not at home—in America.

"A clear-eyed look at the insecurity and yearning for a sense of belonging that are part of the immigrant experience . . . Movingly told." —*The Washington Post Book World*

"Subtle . . . Powerful . . . Reveals the intricacies of family, the impact of culture and place, and the profound power of language." —*The San Diego Tribune*

An Algonquin Readers Round Table Edition with Reading Group Guide and Other Special Features • Fiction • ISBN 978-1-56512-975-7

A Reliable Wife, a novel by Robert Goolrick

Rural Wisconsin, 1907. In the bitter cold, Ralph Truitt stands alone on a train platform anxiously awaiting the arrival of the woman who answered his newspaper ad for "a reliable wife." The woman who arrives is not the one he expects in this *New York Times* #1 bestseller about love and madness, longing and murder.

"[A] chillingly engrossing plot . . . Good to the riveting end."
—*USA Today*

"Deliciously wicked and tense . . . Intoxicating."
—*The Washington Post*

"A rousing historical potboiler." —*The Boston Globe*

An Algonquin Readers Round Table Edition with Reading Group Guide and Other Special Features • Fiction • ISBN-13: 978-1-56512-977-1

Water for Elephants, a novel by Sara Gruen

As a young man, Jacob Jankowski is tossed by fate onto a rickety train, home to the Benzini Brothers Most Spectacular Show on Earth. Amid a world of freaks, grifters, and misfits, Jacob becomes involved with Marlena, the beautiful young equestrian star; her husband, a charismatic but twisted animal trainer; and Rosie, an untrainable elephant who is the great gray hope for this third-rate show. Now in his nineties, Jacob at long last reveals the story of their unlikely yet powerful bonds, ones that nearly shatters them all.

"[An] arresting new novel . . .With a showman's expert timing, [Gruen] saves a terrific revelation for the final pages, transforming a glimpse of Americana into an enchanting escapist fairy tale." —*The New York Times Book Review*

An Algonquin Readers Round Table Edition with Reading Group Guide and Other Special Features • Fiction • ISBN 978-1-56512-560-5

Breakfast with Buddha, a novel by Roland Merullo

When his sister tricks him into taking her guru, a crimson-robed monk, on a trip to their childhood home, Otto Ringling, a confirmed skeptic, is not amused. Six days on the road with an enigmatic holy man who answers every question with a riddle is not what he'd planned. But along the way, Otto is given the remarkable opportunity to see his world—and more important, his life—through someone else's eyes.

"Enlightenment meets *On the Road* in this witty, insightful novel." —*The Boston Sunday Globe*

"A laugh-out-loud novel that's both comical and wise . . . balancing irreverence with insight." —*The Louisville Courier-Journal*

An Algonquin Readers Round Table Edition with Reading Group Guide and Other Special Features • Fiction • ISBN 978-1-56512-616-9

Between Here and April,
a novel by Deborah Copaken Kogan

When a deep-rooted memory suddenly surfaces, Elizabeth Burns becomes obsessed with the long-ago disappearance of her childhood friend April Cassidy.

"The perfect book club book."
—*The Washington Post Book World*

"[A] haunting page-turner . . . [A] compelling look at what it means to be a mother and a wife." —*Working Mother*

"Extraordinary . . . This is a story that needs to be told."
—*Elle*, #1 Reader's Pick

An Algonquin Readers Round Table Edition with Reading Group Guide and Other Special Features • Fiction • ISBN 978-1-56512-932-0

Every Last Cuckoo, a novel by Kate Maloy

In the tradition of Jane Smiley and Sue Miller comes this wise and gratifying novel about a woman who gracefully accepts a surprising new role in life just when she thinks her best years are behind her.

Winner of the ALA Reading List Award for Women's Fiction

"Truly engrossing . . . An excellent book club selection."
—*Library Journal*

"A tender and wise story of what happens when love lasts."
—Katharine Weber, author of *Triangle*

"Inspiring . . . Grabs the reader by the heart."
—*The New Orleans Times-Picayune*

An Algonquin Readers Round Table Edition with Reading Group Guide and Other Special Features • Fiction • ISBN 978-1-56512-675-6

Mudbound, a novel by Hillary Jordan

Mudbound is the saga of the McAllan family, who struggle to survive on a remote ramshackle farm, and the Jacksons, their black sharecroppers. When two men return from World War II to work the land, the unlikely friendship between these brothers-in-arms—one white, one black—arouses the passions of their neighbors. In this award-winning portrait of two families caught up in the blind hatred of a small Southern town, prejudice takes many forms, both subtle and ruthless.

"This is storytelling at the height of its powers . . .
Hillary Jordan writes with the force of a Delta storm."
—Barbara Kingsolver

Winner of the Bellwether Prize for Fiction

An Algonquin Readers Round Table Edition with Reading Group Guide and Other Special Features • Fiction • ISBN 978-1-56512-677-0

Saving the World, a novel by Julia Alvarez

While Alma Huebner is researching a new novel, she discovers the true story of Isabel Sendales y Gómez, who embarked on a courageous sea voyage to rescue the New World from smallpox. The author of *How the García Girls Lost Their Accents* and *In the Time of the Butterflies* captures the worlds of two women living two centuries apart but with surprisingly parallel fates.

"Fresh and unusual and thought-provokingly sensitive."
—*The Boston Globe*

"Engrossing, expertly paced." —*People*

An Algonquin Readers Round Table Edition with Reading Group Guide and Other Special Features • Fiction • ISBN 978-1-56512-558-2

Coal Black Horse, a novel by Robert Olmstead

When Robey Childs's mother has a premonition about her husband fighting in the Civil War, she sends her only son to find him and bring him home. At fourteen, Robey thinks he's off on a great adventure. But it takes the gift of a powerful and noble coal black horse to show him how to undertake the most important journey in his life.

"A remarkable creation." —*Chicago Tribune*

"Exciting . . . A grueling adventure." —*The New York Times Book Review*

An Algonquin Readers Round Table Edition with Reading Group Guide and Other Special Features • Fiction • ISBN 978-1-56512-601-5

An Arsonist's Guide to Writers' Homes in New England,
a novel by Brock Clarke

The past catches up with Sam Pulsifer, the hapless hero of this incendiary novel, when after spending ten years in prison for accidentally burning down Emily Dickinson's house, the homes of other famous new England writers go up in smoke. To prove his innocence, he sets out to uncover the identity of this literary-minded arsonist.

"Funny, profound . . . A seductive book with a payoff on every page." —*People*

"Wildly, unpredictably funny . . . As cheerfully oddball as its title." —*The New York Times*

An Algonquin Readers Round Table Edition with Reading Group Guide and Other Special Features • Fiction • ISBN 978-1-56512-614-5

A Blessing on the Moon, a novel by Joseph Skibell

Hailed by the *New York Times* as "confirmation that no subject lies beyond the grasp of a gifted, committed imagination," this highly acclaimed novel is a magical tale about the Holocaust—a fable inspired by fact. Not since Art Spiegelman's *Maus* has a work so powerfully evoked one of the darkest moments of the twentieth century with such daring originality.

"As magical as it is macabre." —*The New Yorker*

"Hugely enjoyable . . . A compelling tour de force, a surreal but thoroughly accessible page-turner." —*Houston Chronicle*

An Algonquin Readers Round Table Edition with Reading Group Guide and Other Special Features • Fiction • ISBN 978-1-61620-018-3